National Treasure or Trash

War, Memory, and the Intergenerational Costs of Combat

Major (Retired) Michael P. Hart

National Treasure or Trash: War, Memory, and the Intergenerational Costs of Combat

A contemporary view on war, PTSD, and the results on the individual and society/segments that were exposed to combat, violence and associated memories

ISBN#: 979-8-9936439-0-8

By Major Retired Michael P. Hart, MBA, BS, GC-HRM

Publisher's Note & Copyright Page

National Treasure or Trash: War, Memory, and the Intergenerational Cost of Combat

ISBN: 979-8-9936439-0-8 (Paperback / Digital Edition)

Some names, locations, and identifying details have been modified or combined to protect the privacy and security of individuals and their families. Every effort has been made to preserve historical accuracy while safeguarding personal integrity and operational confidentiality.

This work has been written in full accordance with U.S. Department of Defense and U.S. Army regulations governing the disclosure of sensitive, restricted, or classified information. All material referenced herein is declassified, publicly available, or of a historical nature exceeding ten (10) years from the date of any relevant operation or event. All historical references, images, documents, oral histories, and quotations are used solely for educational and scholarly purposes under established fair-use provisions of U.S. copyright law. Every reasonable effort has been made to credit and verify all sources. The interpretations and commentary expressed herein are those of the author and do not necessarily represent the views of any institution, archive, or agency.

Published in the United States by Hart Legacy Press. Printed in the U.S.A. First Edition — 2025

Why National Treasure or Trash?

The title National Treasure or Trash has raised questions since the beginning. Its origin is simple.

In April 2022, during a long conversation with family and friends about the Russian invasion of Ukraine, geopolitics, and the economics of war, someone later described me as — half seriously, half joking—as a "national treasure." The phrase stayed with me, not because it felt flattering, but because it felt unresolved.

Those of us shaped by the Global War on Terror grew up watching planes strike the Twin Towers. We went to war believing in purpose. We watched friends deploy and never return. And in 2021, we watched planes lift off from Bagram as the war ended not with clarity, but with silence. The lessons of that generation—why we went, what violence was demanded, what it cost—did not disappear. They became inconvenient.

Our scars are visible and invisible, carried in plain sight and largely ignored. The experience exists, but the appetite to hear it does not. Praised in passing, thanked in ceremony, and then set aside, the knowledge earned at great cost was neither fully received nor fully rejected.

So, the question remains: are these lessons a national treasure—something to be preserved, learned from, and carried forward—or are they treated as disposable, uncomfortable, and easily discarded? This book lives inside that tension, asking what a society chooses to keep, and what it quietly throws away.

This is not only my story. It is the story of us. It carries truths found in every part of American life—from Veterans of Foreign Wars (VFW) halls to family rooms, from late-night conversations to silences where names are spoken carefully or not at all. This is my family's story, but it is also a fragment of countless others, carried across generations in ways both visible and unseen.

I do not feel as though I wrote this story so much as assembled it. I cannot claim ownership of it, because no single person can. It belongs to those who lived it, those who inherited it, and those still shaped by it without having words for why.

What, then, do we teach our children? Not just history, but inheritance. What we have learned as sons and daughters and now carry as fathers and mothers. Violence must be known—not glorified, not hidden, not simplified. It must be understood for what it does to those who wield it, to those who endure it, and to the societies that choose to use it. To pretend otherwise is not innocence; it is amnesia. And amnesia is how the same lessons are paid for again, by a generation that never asked to relearn them.

Author's Note on Sensitive Content

This work addresses the full reality of war – its violence, trauma, and the long shadows it leaves. Several chapters include frank discussion of combat, moral injury, post-traumatic stress, and suicide. These accounts are not written to shock, but to tell the truth about what war does to people, families, and nations.

If you find any section difficult, step away, take your time, and reach out for support.

No one should have to carry these memories alone.

If you or someone you know is struggling or in crisis:

Veterans Crisis Line (U.S.) – Dial 988, then press 1, or text 838255

988 Suicide & Crisis Lifeline – Dial 988 or visit 988lifeline.org

All services are free, confidential, and available 24 hours a day.

This book is written to honor those who lived, served, and fell – whether on the battlefield or after it. Their stories deserve to be remembered with honesty and respect.

Notes on Sources and Citations

This work was built from memory, record, and reflection — a blend of lived experience, archival study, and the testimony of those who came before me. Readers who wish to explore the sources and documentation in greater depth are encouraged to consult the extensive back matter and references.

The sources span eighty years of material:

Primary records from the U.S. Army Center of Military History, National Archives, Department of Defense, and the Department of Veterans Affairs.

Secondary scholarship from historians, journalists, and veterans who documented the wars they fought and the policies that shaped them.

Cultural works include films, literature, and art — that helped America remember, and sometimes distort, its own story.

Every citation represents either a factual verification or a moral echo: an attempt to connect the human consequences of policy to the individuals who endured them. Whenever firsthand accounts or oral histories are cited, they are presented with respect for privacy and accuracy; I have drawn on both published testimonies and private correspondence entrusted to me by veterans and families.

All interpretations and conclusions remain my own. Wherever official records end, I have sought truth through comparison — weighing memory against evidence, and empathy against detachment. My goal has not been to rewrite history, but to listen more carefully to it.

Major (Ret.) Michael P. Hart

CONTENTS

PART IV - Modern Costs

PART V - Reckoning and Lessons

To those who carried rifles, and to those who carried their memories.

To the veterans who lived, the families who endured, and the children who inherited the silence.

This book is for the ones who stayed — and for the ones who could not.

May we tell their stories with honesty, and may their sacrifices never be rewritten as convenience.

FORWARD

War teaches in fragments. Some lessons we remember. Others we repeat.

This book began as an attempt to connect the dots between those fragments — from Tarawa's surf to Tikrit's sand, from Goettges' patrol to Kabul's gates. I did not set out to write a history of battles, but a ledger of what war leaves behind: the broken rhythms of families, the quiet suicides, the memories that refuse to fade.

I have served with men and women who carried those burdens. Some brought them home. Some did not. Their stories are not statistics. They are the invisible price of service, the unfinished chapters in every generation's war.

National Treasure or Trash is written as both witness and warning. It is not meant to glorify or to condemn, but to remember honestly — to strip away the polish of parades and the politics of convenience, until what remains is truth.

If there is a message here, it is simple: War never truly ends. It only changes form. And what we choose to forget, our children will be forced to learn again.

Major (Ret.) Michael P. Hart

PART I

WWII AND THE MYTH OF THE GREATEST GENERATION

1

THE STORIES WE TELL OURSELVES

The phrase *"Greatest Generation"* was born in the 1990s, crafted to honor Americans who endured the Depression and then won World War II. It was shorthand – a way to bind trauma and triumph into a tidy story. But simplification always comes at a cost. To call them "greatest" risks glossing over the jagged truth: that victory was never inevitable, that violence was brutal, and that the legacies they left were complicated – both noble and scarring.

We like to imagine the war ending neatly in 1945, capped by ticker-tape parades and postwar accords. In reality, it did not end so cleanly. It continued a relationship with violence – one that remains familiar today, not because it is new, but because it was never fully reckoned with. That continuity stretched through reconstruction, the Marshall Plan, the partition of Germany, the Cold War, and eventually Vietnam, where the unresolved contradictions of American power came due.

Parents who had carried rifles in the Pacific or marched across Europe now found themselves leading. These men and women — once the rank and file — had become commanders, policymakers, and parents, while positions of authority were increasingly occupied by seasoned, victorious, and often cynical leaders shaped by World War II. They pushed the nation toward a new kind of war — messy, unpopular, morally gray. Some sent their sons willingly. Others made different choices.

My grandfather William "Wade" Hart, who had fought the Japanese hand-to-hand on Okinawa with the 7th Infantry Division, swore he would not allow his children to fight in Vietnam. That decision did not come from cowardice. It came from love — from scars too deep to pass on.

My great-uncle, Walter Donahue, by contrast, went back. He had served as an X-ray technician with the 45th Field Hospital in Europe, treating the broken bodies of the 101st and later divisions of General Patton's spearhead. He earned five European Campaign Stars and the Silver Star device denoting them. Later, as a doctor, he volunteered to support civilian hospitals near **Quảng Trị** in 1969.

One chose to protect; another to heal. Both choices were shaped by war, both by its horror. This tension — between myth and memory, between survival and service — is what we inherit. **The "Greatest Generation" is not one story. It is thousands. And unless we tell them fully, we learn only half the lesson.**

When memory fades, violence returns — not suddenly, but predictably. The twentieth century proved this with terrible clarity. **World War II** alone touched **nearly three-**

quarters of the planet's population. More than one hundred million men and women were pulled into uniform, and roughly **seventy to eighty-five million people** — Soldiers and civilians alike — **were killed**. Between three and four percent of all human beings alive at the time died as a direct result of the war. **No single event in recorded history has altered humanity more completely.**

And yet, when the war ended in 1945, the world did not absorb its lesson — it turned away from it. The violence had become too vast to process, too familiar to shock. But it was not new, and it did not stop. Even before the war was formally declared, mass death was already underway: Japanese expansion in China and Soviet famine and purges killed an estimated **eight to twelve million people** between **1930 and 1937**, largely **ignored by the world**. After victory V-Day in Europe was declared, the killing continued under the banner of peace. Between **1945 and 1948**, **12 to 14 million ethnic German civilians** were expelled from Eastern Europe; historians estimate **500,000 to 2 million** perished from **starvation, exposure, disease, and reprisals** as entire communities dissolved under forced marches and neglect. At the same time, China slid back into civil war, claiming **another one to two million lives** before **1949.** Soldiers and civilians, victors and vanquished alike, were consumed in silence.

For Americans, that turning away took a particular form. Exhausted by sacrifice and buoyed by distance, the nation rushed toward normalcy rather than reckoning. Families were built at record pace. Suburbs spread. Highways stitched the continent together. Children grew up on westerns and war films that ended cleanly, where courage produced order and the camera cut away before the cost lingered. **Disneyland opened in 1955**, offering a curated fantasy of frontier, heroism, and innocence — a nation remade as spectacle rather than scar. In time, the most destructive war in human history was remembered less as lived terror than as a story with a satisfying ending. Prosperity softened memory. Myth replaced mourning.

The world was exhausted. The scale of the slaughter had broken the capacity to grieve. So, societies chose amnesia — rebuilding cities, redrawing borders, and calling it peace. Violence was no longer aberration; it became background noise. And in that forgetting, the conditions were set for its return — not as something new, but as something already familiar, waiting only for memory to fade.

The Contrast in Peace: Pacific vs. Europe

General MacArthur was not modern by today's standards, but his occupation of Japan was governed by a clear and explicit policy choice: **civilians would not be punished for the crimes of the state**. Under the Supreme Commander for the Allied Powers (SCAP), food security became an immediate priority. U.S. authorities imported millions of tons of grain into a defeated enemy nation that had lost much of its agricultural base and urban infrastructure. Distribution systems were stabilized, black-market seizures were curtailed, and **mass starvation—widely predicted in 1945—was averted**.

This was not cultural inevitability. **It was policy. Collective guilt was explicitly rejected**. Emperor Hirohito was retained not out of sentiment, but to prevent institutional collapse. Democratic reforms were sequenced after survival, not enforced through deprivation. **Political transformation was made possible because the population lived long enough** to experience it.

The **contrast with postwar Germany** is stark. In Europe, early occupation policy operated under a logic of **collective responsibility.** Food shortages were tolerated as moral consequence. Industrial capacity was dismantled faster than civilian relief arrived. In the winters of **1945–47, millions of German civilians** lived at or below subsistence levels, and hundreds of thousands—possibly more—**died from starvation, disease, and exposure** before policy shifted toward recovery. Justice was confused with punishment, and accountability with suffering.

This distinction matters. Democracies do not strengthen themselves by humiliating defeated populations. They preserve legitimacy by separating responsibility from inheritance. MacArthur's Japan demonstrates that **restraint is not weakness—it is statecraft**. Where survival is secured first, democratic order can take root. Where deprivation is used as pedagogy, resentment and instability follow.

2

HARD AND SOFT AMERICA

Every war reveals not just military strength but cultural fault lines. Tocqueville wrote of America's contradictions in the 1830s; later thinkers called it "Hard America" and "Soft America." **Hard America is disciplined**, hierarchical, competitive. **Soft America is nurturing, democratic, forgiving**. Each **generation slides between** these poles, and war magnifies the swing.

For the so-called Greatest Generation, hardness came early: child labor, Depression poverty, strict hierarchies in schools, work, and family. Baby Boomers were raised in the relative comfort of postwar affluence, yet were the ones drafted for Vietnam. Generation X inherited disillusionment — Watergate, stagflation, cultural fragmentation. Millennials, like myself, grew up on John Wayne movies, guitars, and faith, raised on the myths of valor yet living in a softer, consumerist America. Gen Z and Alpha watch wars streamed like games, distant but persistent, their contact with the military mostly through relatives or recruiters at high-school lunch tables.

What does this cultural pendulum mean for warfighters? Simply that each generation fights differently, because each is shaped differently. Children of hardship fight as if survival is instinct. Children of comfort fight with borrowed conviction, sometimes struggling to reconcile ideals with blood.

The Sports Pipeline and the Military Feedback Loop

In the absence of a draft, America's toughness found a new proving ground — the playing field. The same cultural architecture once reserved for military training migrated into locker rooms and stadiums. Coaches became drill instructors; uniforms became gear; fans became spectators and seminary audiences to the mythology of sacrifice. Athletes internalized a code: discipline, teamwork, mission. But over time, the field did more than shape character — it became a recruiting ground.

The **"sports pipeline effect"** extends beyond feeding college programs. It channels social capital, prestige, and institutional trust toward organized athletic institutions, which now often overlap with military influence. High-school and college athletes — especially in football, wrestling, and track — already exhibit many traits the military prizes. In some cases, the next step is marketed as natural. The implication is subtle but powerful: the warrior is already in uniform, just wearing different colors.

That overlap was reinforced by the country's elite educational systems. Ivy League universities, which once trained statesmen and clergy, cultivated parallel notions of leadership through athletics and reserve-officer programs. At the same time, the U.S. service academies — West Point, Annapolis, and the Air Force Academy — absorbed many of the same virtues: competition, excellence, and esprit de corps. Together they formed a dual ladder of prestige, one academic and one martial, both feeding the same national mythology of disciplined success.

Just as these institutions reinforced the sports-to-service ethos, individual figures embodied it. **Dwight D. Eisenhower**, before leading the Allied invasion of Europe, had been a promising halfback for the 1912 Army Cadets. That season culminated in the legendary game against Jim Thorpe's Carlisle Indian Industrial School, later chronicled in Lars Anderson's Carlisle vs. Army: Jim Thorpe, Dwight Eisenhower, **Pop Warner**, and the Forgotten Story of Football's Greatest Battle. The contest was more than sport: it was a collision of two American myths — the disciplined Soldier and the dispossessed warrior. On that field, Eisenhower learned strategy, teamwork, and humility — lessons he would carry to Normandy three decades later.

The Army-Carlisle game revealed that long before global war, America had already fused athletic competition with national identity. Football, with its formations, playbooks, and collisions, mirrored the battlefield; its heroes mirrored generals. From the Ivy League's manicured fields to West Point's parade grounds, the pipeline from sport to service became not an accident but a design — a rehearsal for leadership, obedience, and organized aggression.

That connection became explicit in the post-9/11 era. The **Department of Defense** spent **$53 million** between **2012 and 2015 subsidizing patriotic events in sports** — flyovers, "Salute to Service" games, and military appreciation nights. These weren't simply gestures of gratitude; they were deliberate partnerships between institutions that shaped American identity. The Army conducted a massive investigation into the NASCAR sponsorship of Dale Earnhardt Junior; the question what tangibly did the Army get from these expenditures? By 2024, the NFL alone had raised **$73 million through military-themed campaigns** and yet again the military spent millions more determining if they were effective or not.

Analysts call this concentration of influence a stovepipe effect — where distinct cultural pipelines feed into a single ideological outcome. Athletics, academia, and the armed forces each operate independently, yet all reinforce a shared mythology of service and competition. Energy flows inward — toward the preservation of militarized virtue — but rarely outward, into broader civic engagement or reflection.

In this way, the institutions that once built citizens now manufacture performers. The virtues remain the same — discipline, competition, resilience — but the audience has changed. We no longer cultivate strength for shared survival, but for spectacle. The same traits that once sustained a republic at war now feed an economy of entertainment. Hard America drills the body; Soft America sells it. Between them, the concept of citizenship erodes into careerism. The uniform, whether jersey or camouflage, still carries weight — but the meaning behind it grows lighter with every season.

Lesson: The result is subtle but powerful. The rituals of competition and command persist, but the stakes have changed. Stadiums replaced training grounds; scholarships replaced enlistments. The muscles remain hard, but the meaning has softened.

3

GUADALCANAL, 1942 - THE BARBARITY OF MODERN WAR

Forgotten Lessons

When the Marines came ashore at Guadalcanal, they carried more than rifles. They carried a nation's uncertainty. America had not fought a war like this in decades — the lessons of World War I forgotten, the "Banana Wars" in the Caribbean dismissed as sideshows. Budgets had shrunk; institutional memory had atrophied. They were unprepared.

The lessons forgotten were not only tactical — they were lessons of violence itself. The United States had once learned them at a terrible cost during the Civil War, when industrial killing first met fraternal blood. That generation understood what war did to nations, how it scarred not just Soldiers but whole cities, families, and consciences. Yet those memories faded into sepia and song. By 1942, the Civil War's carnage had become heritage — its horror repackaged as reconciliation.

What was quietly erased was the aftermath. By the **mid-**

1890s, contemporary observers noted that **roughly one-third of Union veterans who had survived the Civil War were already dead**, a mortality rate far beyond what age alone could explain. At **Grand Army of the Republic (GAR)** reunions, speakers and pension officials openly acknowledged that alcohol abuse, untreated psychological wounds, and suicide were claiming veterans at staggering rates. At the **1895 GAR National Encampment**, it was remarked with grim irony that self-destruction and **drink** had **killed more Union veterans after the war than Confederate bullets had during it**. The nation gathered to celebrate reunion while its survivors disappeared into early graves, almshouses, asylums, and saloons.

This was not a failure of character. It was the first American encounter with what we would now recognize as **postwar trauma and moral injury** — long before language existed to name it. The Civil War taught the country how to fight modern war. It also taught, and then forgot, what modern war does to those who survive it.

The silence after the Great War was not only cultural; it was political. When World War I veterans demanded tangible support during the depths of the Great Depression, the nation answered with force instead of care. In **1932**, tens of thousands of veterans — the so-called Bonus Army — marched on Washington seeking early payment of a promised service bonus so they could feed their families. Rather than relief, they were met by U.S. Army troops. Under the direction of Douglas MacArthur, active-duty Soldiers used cavalry, bayonets, and tear gas to drive veterans from the capital and burn their camps. The message was unmistakable: honor was ceremonial, obligation deferred. The nation that had sent them into the trenches now treated their demands as disorder rather than debt. America did not draw closer to its veterans after the Great War — it pushed them back into silence.

What these moments reveal is not only how nations forget, but where consequence is ultimately forced to land when they do.

Modern war involves millions, but it repeatedly turns on the actions of very few. Not because those individuals are extraordinary, but because systems compress consequence downward. Empires mobilize populations; moments decide outcomes. A patrol, a pilot, a lieutenant, a commander — each operating with partial information and no sense of scale — becomes the hinge on which lives, cities, and futures turn.

What matters, then, is not brilliance in the moment, but preparation before it. What lessons has this person learned about violence before they are asked to wield it? Have they been taught restraint, responsibility, and the cost of action — or only efficiency, obedience, and speed? When consequence collapses onto one set of hands, it is prior formation, not intention, that determines what follows.

This is not an exception in history. It is the pattern.

Small Wars, Forgotten Lessons

Between the great wars, the nation fought smaller ones — so-called "minor engagements" that, in scale and savagery, foreshadowed the conflicts to come. From Nicaragua and Haiti to the Philippines and China, Marines and Soldiers relearned lessons in jungle warfare, ambush, counterinsurgency, and occupation that would later reappear in Vietnam, and again in the deserts and cities of the Global War on Terror (GWOT). Between **1898 and 1934**, the United States conducted more than **two dozen overseas military intervention**s, often involving prolonged occupation and sustained violence against irregular forces and civilian populations. These were not brief police actions; in places like the Philippines alone, hundreds of thousands of civilians died during counterinsurgency campaigns that blurred the line between combatant and noncombatant.

One episode was especially instructive — and largely forgotten. During the Philippine-American War, U.S. forces attempting to suppress guerrilla resistance on the island of Samar resorted to collective punishment. Villages were burned. Food supplies were destroyed. The island was ordered turned into a "howling wilderness." The campaign killed **tens of thousands of Filipino civilians**, many through starvation and disease rather than direct fire. Officers debated the morality of such measures even as they employed them. The lesson was clear at the time: occupation breeds resistance, resistance invites escalation, and escalation corrodes restraint. The lesson did not endure.

And so, the pattern repeated. Each generation assumed its war would be different — that new technology, better intentions, or moral clarity would spare it from the old dynamics. By the time the Marines landed on Guadalcanal, the country had forgotten what total war demanded. Violence had been concentrated within a relatively small, professional military — the product of postwar drawdowns and career forces — insulating the broader society from its cost. That insulation fostered the belief that violence could be directed, managed, and contained: another instrument of policy, not the failure of it. The broader nation remained deeply isolationist, convinced that it lacked both the appetite and obligation for sustained war — an assumption shared by Japan and much of the world. Guadalcanal proved otherwise.

Lesson: Violence does not negotiate; it multiplies. It consumes the just and unjust alike.

The Goettge Patrol

The Marines who stepped ashore on Guadalcanal carried courage — and the burden of rediscovery. Every mistake they made had been made before. Every ambush, every casualty, every night attack reminded them that war has no memory, only repetition.

Colonel Frank Goettge, a respected intelligence officer, led a reconnaissance team of roughly 25 Marines, a Navy corpsman, and an interpreter into the jungle west of Henderson Field on August 12, 1942. They went in believing the war might still be negotiated — that Japanese forces were starving, demoralized, and willing to surrender. That belief was not naïveté; it was inheritance. It reflected American assumptions formed in earlier wars, where encirclement eventually produced capitulation.

Instead, the patrol walked into a perfectly prepared ambush.

Gunfire erupted at close range. Marines fought on until their weapons jammed or their ammunition ran out. Survivors were hunted down individually in the darkness. Nearly every man in the patrol was killed. Their bodies were left unburied, consumed by insects and jungle rot, many mutilated with swords. Days later, Marine patrols found the remains intentionally left where they would be discovered — a message as much as an act of war.

It was not just a tactical disaster. It was a psychological rupture.

The assumption that this war would resemble previous wars died with the patrol. The Japanese would not surrender. They would infiltrate at night, feign death, attack wounded Marines, and fight to annihilation. Guadalcanal was not a campaign of maneuver; it was a campaign of endurance, terror, and mutual exhaustion. Marines learned to fight while malnourished, diseased, and sleepless — surviving on captured rice, quinine, and sheer will. This was not combat as Americans understood it. It was something older, darker, and more absolute.

Rediscovering Barbarity

Richard Tregaskis's *Guadalcanal Diary* carried that reality home without varnish. He wrote of the stench of decomposing bodies, the fear of night attacks, and the constant attrition from malaria, dysentery, and jungle rot. Men were evacuated not because they were wounded, but because their bodies simply gave out. Combat was inseparable from sickness. Survival was as much about resisting decay as resisting the enemy.

Later, Hollywood would transform this experience into myth. Films like *Sands of Iwo Jima* distilled chaos into courage and suffering into purpose. But the myth was purchased at terrible cost. Behind every lesson learned lay blood: the rediscovery of amphibious doctrine under fire, logistics under bombardment, leadership under terror, and discipline when fear was constant and rest was impossible.

None of this was new. The Marine Corps had known these truths before — in the Philippines, in Haiti, in Nicaragua. They had been written down, debated, and then quietly shelved in peacetime. Guadalcanal forced their return. The Corps did not innovate so much as remember — relearning what war demands when it strips away illusion. It relearned it the only way armies ever do: through ambushes, graves, and men who did not come back.

War Remembered and Reimagined

When Terrence Malick released *The Thin Red Line* in 1998, he returned to Guadalcanal not as historian but as a poet. His film was a meditation on nature, fear, and the human spirit — a haunting elegy filmed with beauty that bordered on contradiction. Malick's lens lingered on grass, water, and sunlight, searching for God in the noise of artillery. Yet even with its masterful cinematography and ensemble cast — Sean Penn, Nick Nolte,

Jim Caviezel — the film could not capture what the Goettge Patrol had endured. Its silence was eloquent but bloodless, its beauty deliberate but detached. It touched the soul of war but missed its smell.

In contrast, Steven Spielberg's *Saving Private Ryan*, released the same year, spoke with a different tongue — the roar of chaos. Its opening sequence at Omaha Beach became the defining cinematic vision of the "Greatest Generation": brutal, visceral, righteous. Spielberg's realism was not poetry but testimony. Where *The Thin Red Line* asked why men fight, Saving Private Ryan answered with how they die. Together, they mark the boundaries of memory: Malick's meditation on the soul and Spielberg's hymn to sacrifice — one seeking meaning, the other asserting it.

The Geometry of Destruction

History did not end on that island; it reset. Every generation since has been forced to relearn the same arithmetic of violence under new names. In Vietnam, Soldiers patrolled jungles that looked like echoes of Guadalcanal's thickets. In Fallujah, Marines cleared houses the way their grandfathers had cleared trenches. In Ukraine, artillery pounds cities that once hosted peace accords. The uniforms and rhetoric change, but the geometry of destruction remains constant.

We keep inventing new tools for old habits, mistaking technology for wisdom. Every century promises it has learned restraint; every century proves otherwise.

Lesson: Every new war begins with a salute to the last — and ends with a whisper of the same regrets.

The Language of Targets

The barbarity was not limited to combat. National sentiment, hardened into national will and stoked by propaganda, blurred the line between enemy and animal. The enemy was reduced to caricature — slime, subhuman, "oriental." Skulls and bones of Japanese Soldiers were mailed home as trophies. *Life* magazine once published a photograph of a smiling American woman posing beside a skull sent to her by her fiancé. PFC Wade Hart's tent on Saipan had a Japanese skull nailed at the entrance. At the time, it was taken as proof of victory. Today, it reads as proof of moral erosion.

A simpler illustration lies closer to home.

On most Army ranges, the targets are green — man-sized silhouettes, faceless and anonymous. They rise, fall, and disappear on command: a mechanical echo of what was once flesh and fear. We call them targets or silhouettes, nothing more. Officially, the color was chosen for visibility and contrast. Unofficially, it does something deeper. Green has become the safe color of killing.

It was not always this clean.

That is the quiet legacy of every generation's war. We never stop naming the enemy — *Krauts, Japs, gooks, Charlie, hajis* — but we never stop abstracting him. Whether through a racial slur or a geometric silhouette, the purpose is the same: to make the enemy less real than the man holding the rifle. Somewhere between the training range and the battlefield, a line blurs — between enemy and target, between Soldier and survivor.

Today, that separation is built directly into training.

Green silhouettes appear at distances from 25 to 300 meters. They expose for a fixed time, then drop. Soldiers must hit a prescribed number — 21 of 40, 23 of 40 — to qualify. The drill teaches speed, accuracy, and muscle memory. It also teaches something quieter: that hesitation kills, that targets are meant to fall, and that what falls is not to be dwelled on.

The faceless green shapes accomplish what language once did. They remove identity. They remove story. They create distance.

Doctrine has improved. Discipline has improved. But the underlying truth remains: war has always required some form of abstraction. The difference now is that abstraction no longer sounds like hatred. It looks like efficiency.

And efficiency, too, has a cost.

Lesson: The jungle did not just consume bodies. It consumed certainties — about mercy, about civilization, and about what it meant to be human under the pressure of endless killing.

Fix Bayonets!

My grandfather, Wade Hart, used to warn me, "Michael Patrick, it's the artillery you don't hear that you have to worry about."

He had learned that lesson the hard way, under the thunder of Okinawa's guns. Before I deployed to Afghanistan, he shared those fragments of wisdom — not lectures, but quiet truths delivered in the same jovial manner of Soldiers talking amongst themselves. He never romanticized war. He spoke about it the way a man talks about the weather — something larger than himself, something you endure rather than conquer.

He told me about one encounter his unit had on Okinawa — a group of Japanese Soldiers they had wiped out across a ridge; not with rifles, but with spears. As a child, I could hardly believe it. Spears belonged to ancient history, not to men in khaki fighting under artillery and aircraft. It sounded like a campfire story, the kind you nod at politely but tuck away as exaggeration.

Years later, while researching the Pacific campaigns, I found proof that made my stomach turn. First-hand accounts from Marines and Soldiers, photographs from the aftermath, they showed the same thing my grandfather had described: Japanese dead clutching improvised spears. The Japanese field manual confirmed it in cold detail — instructions for cutting a length of bamboo, splitting one end, and binding a bayonet in place with wire or twine when ammunition was gone.

As a child I thought it impossible. As an adult, it is gut-wrenching. It means the enemy my grandfather faced had been reduced to fighting with bamboo and bayonets against tanks, flamethrowers, and machine guns. It also means those last charges were not madness alone, but desperation — men fighting with whatever they had left, determined to die within reach of the enemy.

When he told me those stories before I left for Afghanistan, I didn't yet understand what he meant when he said, "It's the ones you don't hear that you need to worry about." Only after standing at an outpost in Ghazni Province, that I would learn that lesson personally mortars land without an audible warning — a dull cough maybe, a pause, and then impact. Rockets you can sometimes see or hear; I had heard rockets actually whiz over my location on our main base; mortars however they give you nothing. The ones you don't hear are the ones that matter.

I found his words to be painfully true: the unseen and the unheard are what haunt you. You wait for the next thud, counting the seconds between explosions, realizing that fear isn't noise — it's the absence of it. In those moments, I understood what he had meant across decades and wars: that silence is not peace, but the breath before chaos.

The hand-to-hand carnage he described strips away any illusion of clean war. When steel meets bamboo, when riflemen meet men with spears, when mortars fall unseen, civilization itself is only inches thick.

The Pacific war did not wait for Wade to discover brutality on their own following; it trained them for it. Indoctrination against the Japanese enemy was constant and explicit. What we would now describe as grotesque was presented as necessary, even practical. The enemy was framed as incapable of surrender, treacherous by nature, and undeserving of mercy. That belief was reinforced not only by doctrine, but by experience.

On Saipan, prior to landing on Okinawa, Wade's unit conducted nightly ambushes during mop-up operations, honing their combat skills in the field. Between patrols, they wrote letters home from a tent whose entrance was marked by the skull of a Japanese Soldier nailed above it. It was not hidden. It was not questioned. It was understood. The skull served as a warning, a talisman, and a form of psychological armor. It marked a boundary already crossed — a sign that the war had stripped away the last expectation of restraint. In that environment, such acts were not viewed as aberrations. They were part of the landscape, as normal as foxholes and ration tins.

This was the world in which Wade learned to move, to survive, and to fight.

Prisoners, if and when they were taken at all, were rare. Japanese doctrine discouraged surrender, and American Soldiers were trained to distrust it. When captives were secured, they were handled quickly and deliberately. Wade learned how to move prisoners, how to separate them, how to compel cooperation when language, fear, and ideology made trust impossible. This was not cruelty for its own sake. It was procedure born of exhaustion and danger.

Wade never told these stories with pride. He told them as facts. The skull on the tent. The methods used to control prisoners. These were not moments he returned to — they were moments that returned to him. They were not signs of individual savagery, but evidence of a war that had already erased the space between survival and desecration.

Only then does the meaning of his later warning come into focus: that war teaches silence first, and brutality second. That by the time the guns fall quiet, the real damage has already been done.

Lesson: War always regresses toward its primitive core. Even surrounded by technology, it ends the same way—one human being trying to survive another at arm's length.

4

NORMANDY: LIBERATION AND SHADOW

The beaches of Normandy are remembered as shrines to valor. Utah, Omaha, Gold, Juno, Sword — names that conjure sacrifice, unity, liberation. Each June, veterans are paraded through villages that still wave Allied flags. Museums preserve Pegasus Bridge, a paratrooper mannequin dangles from the church steeples in Sainte-Mère-Église, and tourists take selfies among the crosses at Colleville-sur-Mer. Free leaders from around the world have traveled to pay homage to the sacrifices. Nearly all US Presidents have made the pilgrimage to Normandy. President (Former) Joe Biden, having made the trip and spoke from the cliffs of Pointe du Hoc on the 80th Anniversary of D-Day 1944-2024.

Yet beneath the celebration lies grief. Normandy was not only a battlefield of Soldiers but also of civilians. Twenty thousand French civilians died during the campaign, most by Allied bombs meant to clear the way. Caen was leveled; Saint-Lô became "the capital of ruins." Liberation meant rubble, families lost, centuries-old towns erased.

The bocage — hedgerows (overgrown foliage between roads and fields often around or over stone or built berms) that turned fields into fortresses — made fighting slow, intimate, savage. Mercy was rare. SS troops often executed prisoners; Allied units, hardened by losses, often responded in kind. We see it hinted at in Hollywood — *"Band of Brothers"* dramatizing hedgerow fighting — and in nonfiction, such as American Nightingale, the true story of LT. Frances Slanger, the first American nurse killed by enemy fire in Europe. My great-uncle Walter, who served with the 45th Field Hospital, was deeply affected by her death. It was a reminder that even healers were not spared. Official histories soften this; veterans' memoirs do not.

Collateral damage was not incidental. It was strategy. Bombers flattened villages to break German lines. Was Caen's destruction necessary? Could Falaise have been taken with less fire? These questions remain, whispered in Normandy to this day.

The scale of that destruction is often hidden beneath the triumphal story. **Caen**, a city of **60,000**, lost nearly three-quarters of its buildings and more than **3,000 civilians**. **Saint-Lô**, reduced to rubble, lost almost **3,000** of its **12,000** residents. **Lisieux** saw some **800 civilians killed** in a single night of bombing. In the **Falaise Pocket**, whole villages vanished under artillery and air attack. In total, roughly **20,000 French civilians died** in the **Normandy** campaign — most from Allied fire. Their deaths were **not accidental**. They were the **cost of** clearing a path for **liberation.**

What is less remembered is how that destruction looked

on the ground. By 1944, much of the German Army's logistics were still horse-drawn. Thousands of horses pulled artillery, ammunition wagons, food carts, and medical supplies through the Norman countryside. When Allied air power closed the Falaise Pocket, it did not simply destroy armored columns — it pulverized an entire moving ecosystem of men, animals, and equipment. Bombs and artillery turned roads into charnel corridors. Horses and Soldiers were torn apart together, wagons splintered, steel twisted into heaps, bodies left tangled in harness and wreckage. The summer heat finished what the fire began. The stench of decay spread across the fields as an entire encircled army was systematically annihilated from the air and ground.

That reality is only faintly alluded to in war films that pause on the aftermath rather than the charge — the silence after movement, the ruined roads littered with the remains of men and animals alike. Victory there was not cinematic. It was putrefaction and abandonment, paid for long after the front moved east.

This dual memory defines Normandy. For the world, it is triumph — the moment democracy stormed ashore and fascism began to crumble. For those who lived there, it is also loss: of homes pulverized, of families buried beneath rubble, of innocence burned away by liberation itself. To tell only the first story is to preserve myth. To hold both is to tell the truth — that even the most just wars exact their price from those who never chose them.

To **walk those beaches today is to walk between two truths: freedom was bought not only with Allied**

blood, but also with the lives of thousands of civilians whose sacrifices were deemed collateral to the liberation of France. The lesson is not to diminish the valor of the liberators, but to tell the full story — that war, even at its noblest, carries shadows that parades cannot erase.

Walter Donahue entered the war not with a rifle, but with an X-ray machine. He served as a radiology technician in the 45th Field Hospital during the Second World War, where medicine and war collided in ways no manual could prepare him for. He landed on the beaches of Normandy on 10 June under shellfire and went straight into the thick of it, supporting the 101st at Sainte-Mère-Elise. It was there, in France, that he worked alongside Lt. Frances Slanger, the Army nurse later immortalized in Bob Welch's American Nightingale. Slanger was known for her warmth and humor amid exhaustion, for writing letters to Soldiers who had no one else to write them back.

When artillery struck their unit near Elbeuf in October 1944, she became the first American nurse killed by enemy fire in Europe. By this point in the war, Walter was a finely tuned reader of X-rays — not just trained, but experienced. He had seen enough to recognize patterns of damage, to know instinctively when a case would not end well. His training kept him moving through the process, hands steady even when the outcome was certain. He was the one who X-rayed the shrapnel in her back only minutes earlier — an image burned into his memory. It gave him the unique horror of seeing exactly what the artillery had done to his dying friend: shrapnel in her spine and elsewhere. As he looked at the glowing film, he could see the terrible damage in real time — the body of compassion itself broken by war. She died on that operating table. Walt told me this story himself. It is true. He never forgot the quiet way she carried pain, or how she refused to let war strip her of compassion.

Years later, after the war, Walter would become an obstetrician — turning his wartime experience of injury and loss into a vocation for life and renewal. Where war had once brought him images of torn bodies and shattered bone, his postwar years became about delivering children and restoring what conflict had broken. But his service didn't end in hospitals at home. In 1968, at the height of the fighting in Vietnam, he volunteered with the American Medical Association (AMA) and its charter organization Volunteer Physicians for Vietnam. Serving there from October 1968 through December 1969 near **Quảng Trị**, one of the war's most heavily shelled provinces. There, amid tents and bombed-out clinics, he practiced a kind of medicine that was equal parts science and faith — treating civilians caught between armies, delivering babies under the sound of artillery, and tending the wounded in a place where there were no sides left to take. He published numerous articles for use for future doctors and clinics on enhancing mortality rates for both children and mother under these conditions.

His path was the mirror opposite of my Wade's. Where he withdrew from the noise of battle, chaos and uncertainty, outside of ensuring his children would not go to Vietnam, Walter walked into it — not out of defiance, but out of conviction. He had seen what indifference could cost. He had held the X-ray of a dying nurse who refused to abandon her humanity, and he carried that image with him for the rest of his life. In him, I see the living thread that connects American Nightingale to Bob Welch's later work "Pebble in the Water": the belief that a single act of mercy, no matter how small, can send ripples through history

Walter's story is not about glory or recognition. It is about endurance — about a man who chose compassion in a century that rewarded cruelty. His life reminds me that heroism is not always measured by victory, but by the refusal to let war decide who we become. He lived and died quietly, far from the spotlight, but the echo of what he did — the ripple of that single "pebble in the water" — continues outward still.

5

HITLER, STALIN, MAO – THE MACHINERY OF MURDER

The Holocaust is often reduced to numbers — **six million Jews, eleven to twelve million total victims** when one includes Romani, Poles, Soviet POWs, dissidents, the disabled, and LGBTQ people. But numbers flatten what was, in **truth, a system: a modern state converting bureaucracy, propaganda, and industrial efficiency into instruments of extermination.** What began with laws and boycotts became ghettos, transports, and gas chambers. Trains ran on schedule; clerks filled out forms; ashes were cataloged and dumped in rivers.

Before the gas chambers came the guns. The **Einsatzgruppen** — mobile killing units drawn from the SS, Gestapo, and ordinary German police — followed the Wehrmacht into the east after the invasion of the Soviet Union in 1941. Their orders were simple: secure the rear areas, eliminate "enemies of the Reich," and leave no witnesses. They surrounded villages, forced Jews, communists, and Roma into ravines and forests, and shot them in groups. What began as "security operations" became open-air extermination. At **Babi Yar near Kyiv**, over **33,000** people were **murdered in two days. By the end of 1943, more than 1.3 million men, women, and children had been killed by bullets.**

These killings were not the work of monsters but of men with titles and pay stubs – policemen, clerks, teachers, reservists – ordinary people who turned law into murder. The Einsatzgruppen tested what became the template of genocide: administrative orders, logistical precision, and moral vacancy. Every bullet required paperwork. Every corpse was counted. When gas vans and camps replaced bullets, the method changed, but the psychology remained – obedience presented as duty, atrocity disguised as administration.

Even before the camps, the world had been warned. In **1937**, the Imperial Japanese Army entered **Nanking**. Over the next six weeks an estimated **200,000 to 300,000** civilians and prisoners of war were slaughtered; tens of thousands of women were raped. Western journalists filed stories, missionaries smuggled out photographs – and the world largely looked away. Newspapers described it as an "Oriental problem."

Diplomats urged restraint, not outrage. The silence was not ignorance; it was convenience. It revealed how deeply racism had shaped Western perception of whose suffering mattered. When violence happens to "others," it is easier to mistake atrocity for disorder.

Inherited Ideals

Ideals are the soil from which every generation grows. They can nourish, or they can poison, depending on what we plant and how honestly, we tend them. The citizens who filled the rallies of Nuremberg, Moscow, and Beijing did not see themselves as villains. They believed they were upholding the ideals of their fathers — unity, discipline, sacrifice, faith in the state. Those ideals had been passed down through schools, pulpits, and family tables, reinforced by slogans that sounded noble but demanded obedience over conscience.

Every nation teaches its children what it values. The danger comes when those lessons go unexamined. The same virtues that sustain a people in crisis — loyalty, pride, and duty — can become chains when stripped of humility. A child raised to salute without question will grow into an adult who cannot tell the difference between service and submission. A generation taught that its suffering makes it superior will find enemies wherever it looks.

The most terrible regimes of the twentieth century were not built by ignorance alone. They were built by conviction — by men and women who believed they were continuing a noble legacy. They inherited their parents' courage, but not their caution. They learned discipline but not doubt. And so, ideals meant to protect humanity were weaponized against it.

In every century, this inheritance repeats. It is easy to hand our children symbols — flags, slogans, prayers. It is harder to teach them the questions that must accompany those symbols. What does this stand for? Whom does it exclude? What line should never be crossed, no matter the reason? If we cannot pass down those questions, then we pass down only the machinery — not the morality — of our ideals.

Extremes Within: When Movements Are Hijacked

No ideology begins as genocide. It begins with belonging. Most of the men and women who joined fascist, communist, or nationalist movements did not set out to kill. They set out to believe. They were searching for meaning after humiliation, purpose after chaos, certainty after fear. In every generation, those hungriest for order are the most vulnerable to anyone promising it.

The pattern repeats. Every movement begins with moderates and ends with zealots. The well-intentioned create the stage; the fanatics seize the microphone. What starts as unity becomes uniformity. What starts as patriotism becomes purification.

In postwar Germany, the Nazi Party began as a fringe of embittered veterans — men nursing defeat and dreaming of renewal after the armistice of **1918**. Hitler did not rise from the gutter; he was lifted from it. In **1919**, Captain Karl Mayr, a German Army intelligence officer, discovered him and sent him to observe a small political club meeting in a Munich beer hall. There, railway worker Anton Drexler saw his talent and welcomed him in. Playwright Dietrich Eckart polished him — teaching cadence, gesture, and myth. What began as mentorship soon became manipulation.

By **1923**, Hitler had staged his failed Beer Hall Putsch; by **1933**, he was chancellor of Germany. Within a decade, his fringe had captured the core institutions of the state. The courts, the police, the press, and the schools surrendered one after another. Bureaucracy became belief.

When Germany invaded the Soviet Union in **June 1941**, those same institutions produced the Einsatzgruppen — mobile killing units of police, SS, and clerks turned executioners. Between **1941 and 1943**, across occupied Eastern Europe, they murdered more than a million Jews, Roma, and Soviet civilians in open fields and ravines, often by bullet before the gas chambers existed.

The men who carried out those massacres had once filed reports, stamped orders, and saluted flags. What had begun in a Munich beer hall ended in Babi Yar. A movement that promised discipline had mutated into organized savagery, and those who had sworn to serve the people learned to murder them instead.

The same dynamic played out elsewhere. In the Soviet Union, the revolution that began in **1917** in the name of equality turned inward by the late **1930s** during Stalin's Great Purge. Revolutionaries became suspects, comrades became corpses. Loyalty became a moving target, and safety was measured by how quickly one could accuse another. Fear replaced ideology; survival replaced belief.

In China, Mao's Red Guards began as students urged to protect the revolution from corruption during the **Cultural**

Revolution (1966–1976). Within months, they were beating their teachers to death and destroying the history they claimed to honor. The pursuit of purity devoured the very idea of progress.

In Cambodia, **Pol Pot's Khmer Rouge** promised equality and delivered annihilation. Beginning in **1975**, they emptied cities, murdered the educated, and even executed those who wore eyeglasses — a symbol, they claimed, of bourgeois contamination. By the time Vietnamese forces toppled the regime in **1979**, nearly two million Cambodians were dead. Their revolution achieved the ultimate abstraction: a country of graves, managed by accountants of death.

Across nations and ideologies, the story is the same. Every one of these movements began with people who believed they could manage the radicals — that the extremism was temporary, the rhetoric performative, the violence containable. They were wrong. Once purity becomes policy, it no longer needs enemies outside its walls; it manufactures them within. When ideology replaces empathy, extermination becomes administration.

Lesson: Every movement carries within it the seed of its own corruption. When conviction goes unquestioned, when leaders become infallible, and when obedience is mistaken for faith, the fringe becomes the future. The surest defense against tyranny is not strength or order, but doubt — the kind of doubt that asks whether righteousness has started to sound too easy.

Modern Echo: The Return of Political Violence

This is not uncharted territory in American history — but it is a return to one the nation believed it had outgrown. Political violence was once a recurring feature of American life. Between the Civil War and World War I, the United States experienced waves of assassinations, lynchings, labor bombings, and armed political clashes. Four sitting presidents were assassinated. Dozens of governors, mayors, judges, and labor leaders were killed. Entire communities lived with the expectation that politics could turn lethal.

That pattern reappeared violently in the 1960s, when the assassinations of **John F. Kennedy, Malcolm X, Martin Luther King Jr., and Robert F. Kennedy** shattered any remaining illusion that modern America was immune to political murder. For a brief period, violence returned to the center of civic life, exposing how fragile restraint truly was.

What followed was unusual. From the late **1960s through the** early **2000s**, political **violence sharply declined**. Assassinations became rare. Domestic terrorism, while present, was broadly condemned and institutionally contained. For roughly half a century, the United States experienced an anomalous period in which political disagreement was intense but generally restrained. That restraint was not accidental; it was enforced culturally, institutionally, and morally.

That era is ending.

In the past decade, the scale and visibility of political

violence in the United States has risen dramatically. Threats against members of Congress and federal officials have more than doubled since 2016, reaching historic highs. **Following the 2020 election, nearly one in three election officials reported harassment, threats, or intimidation, with many leaving public service altogether.** Armed threats against judges, school boards, and local officials — once unthinkable — are now routine enough to require permanent security measures. According to conflict-tracking data, politically motivated violent incidents in the United States have **increased several-fold since 2019**, driven largely by lone actors radicalized through online grievance ecosystems rather than organized movements.

This escalation mirrors patterns seen abroad. Global conflict monitors report a significant rise in assassination attempts, politically motivated attacks, and threats against public officials worldwide over the last five years. What unites these incidents is not ideology, but method: individuals acting alone, fueled by absolutist narratives that frame violence as moral necessity rather than moral failure.

The danger is not only physical. It is moral. When violence re-enters politics, it does so first as justification. Language shifts. Opponents become enemies. Enemies become obstacles. And obstacles, eventually, become targets. When citizens begin to excuse or cheer the silencing of a voice they dislike, they accept the core logic of tyranny — that violence is legitimate if it serves their side.

American history shows where these leads. Not collapse overnight, but corrosion — slow, normalized, and rationalized.

The lesson of the past century is not that political violence is unprecedented. It is that restraint is fragile, and once lost, extraordinarily difficult to restore.

Lesson: The tools change — rifles replaced by algorithms, mobs by followers — but the temptation is the same. When we abandon restraint, we trade civilization for impulse. The modern echo of political assassination reminds us that democracy survives only when words remain stronger than weapons. Extremism is not a foreign contagion; it is a mutation of our own ideals. It grows from virtues left unexamined — loyalty without conscience, unity without compassion, pride without humility. The most dangerous enemies of a society are never the ones at its borders, but the ones who convince its citizens that cruelty is duty and obedience is virtue.

Indochina: The Next Cycle of Hell

After 1975, Southeast Asia repeated the pattern. In Cambodia, **Pol Pot's Khmer Rouge** declared "Year Zero." They emptied cities, executed intellectuals, and turned rice paddies into killing fields. **Over 1.7 million Cambodians** — roughly **one in five — died** between **1975 and 1979** through execution, starvation, and disease. In neighboring Laos and Vietnam, **another two to three million** perished in civil wars and bombing campaigns that dropped more ordnance than all of World War II combined.

From Nanking's silence to the Cambodian fields, the West's selective empathy formed a grim pattern: outrage when victims looked familiar, detachment when they did not. Racism and distance fed apathy; apathy became permission. Atrocity needs that silence as much as it needs bullets.

Lesson: Mass atrocity is never spontaneous. It is built step by step — through slogans, bureaucracy, and the **quiet consent of those who decide that some lives count less than others.** The warning is not for yesterday. It is for today.

Allegories of Horror: Art, Film, and the Memory of Atrocity

History keeps the record; art keeps the conscience. After the tribunals, artists and filmmakers were left to translate numbers back into emotion — to force audiences to feel what statistics anesthetize.

Bradbury's *Fahrenheit 451* and Truffaut's film imagined a world where books burn and thought itself is outlawed — a descendant of Nazi censorship and Stalinist repression. George Romero's *Night of the Living Dead* turned mindless hunger into metaphor: a nation devouring itself. Its Black protagonist survives the undead only to die by the ignorance of the living, a mirror held to America's own racial violence.

In the twenty-first century, Danny Boyle carried that allegory forward. His *28 Days Later* (2002) and *28 Weeks Later* (2007) — with a long-anticipated *28 Months Later* — shows what happens after the machinery of civilization collapses. The "rage virus" spreads faster than infection; it is fear made flesh. Boyle's London is not fantasy, but regression. Power grids fail, armies fracture, and humanity reverts to instinct. What remains are primal hierarchies — strength, territory, survival — and the uneasy flicker of conscience. His films are studies in de-evolution: how quickly order unravels when memory, ethics, and empathy erode.

Yet even in that descent, Boyle threads a glimmer of humanity. Characters hesitate, choose mercy, or fail to — proof that conscience never dies completely. The real terror is not the infected; it is recognizing how close we all stand to becoming them.

A single image ties the old atrocities to this new allegory: the skull. From the Khmer Rouge's bone fields to the trophies of Pacific battlefields, from mass graves to cinematic ruins, skulls recur as the most honest monument war ever builds. They remind us that beneath every uniform, ideology, or infection lies the same architecture of bone — proof that the distance between victim and survivor is only luck and circumstance.

Across decades and genres, from Truffaut's burning books to Boyle's burning cities, art keeps returning to the same warning: civilization is a thin veneer stretched over our oldest instincts. When fear replaces empathy and obedience replaces thought, the veneer cracks, and the skulls remind us what waits beneath.

Lesson: Art cannot redeem atrocity, but it can hold the mirror steady. It shows us that forgetting is the first contagion, and that humanity's survival depends not on strength but on remembering what it means to be human.

Hollywood and the Pentagon — A Partnership in Narrative Control

For more than **eighty years, Hollywood** and the **U.S. military** have shared a quiet **alliance**—one built on access, image, and influence. From **World War II to Afghanistan**, the Pentagon has helped shape the stories America tells itself about war. Sometimes the partnership is overt: full cooperation in exchange for aircraft, ships, or uniforms. Sometimes it is subtle: a phone call, a note on a script, a line revised to preserve institutional dignity. **But in every era, the arrangement has served a single purpose—to ensure that the nation's self-image as both victim and victor remains intact.**

The relationship truly began during the Second World War. The Office of War Information (OWI) established a Bureau of Motion Pictures that worked directly with studios to review scripts, edit footage, and coordinate messaging. The story of that collaboration is captured in *Five Came Back*—Mark Harris's history and the 2017 documentary that followed five celebrated directors into uniform. John Ford filmed *Midway*'s smoke and chaos; Frank Capra turned enemy propaganda into *Why We Fight*; William Wyler climbed aboard B-17s to shoot *Memphis Belle*; George Stevens entered Dachau with his camera still rolling; John Huston reconstructed the psychological wounds of Soldiers in *Let There Be Light*. Their work proved that cameras could mobilize a democracy as effectively as rifles.

Five Came Back also revealed the cost. Those filmmakers

returned changed—haunted by what their lenses had recorded and what their government had asked them to omit. They had created a national mythology that was both truthful and curated: courage elevated, doubt edited out. Hollywood and Washington discovered together that patriotism sold tickets, and tickets built morale.

The Cold War kept the partnership alive. As communism replaced fascism, Hollywood provided the moral theater for containment. *The Green Berets* (1968), co-directed by John Wayne and produced with Pentagon cooperation, reframed the Vietnam War as noble crusade even as body bags returned home by the thousands. Behind the scenes, scripts that portrayed the military unfavorably were denied access to bases, aircraft, or consultation. Control did not require censorship; it only required scarcity. If a filmmaker wanted realism, cooperation was the price.

After Vietnam fractured the nation's faith in itself, the Pentagon quietly re-engineered its relationship with Hollywood. By the 1980s, *Top Gun* rebuilt the military's image for a new generation, and Navy recruitment soared. The same formulas reappeared in the Gulf War era—sleek hardware, stoic courage, sanitized consequence. Cameras captured glory, not aftermath.

That partnership continues into the modern era. Blockbusters such as *Black Hawk Down*, *Zero Dark Thirty*, and *Lone Survivor* were all produced with Pentagon or service-branch collaboration. Assistance came with expectations: no war crimes, no institutional failures, no ambiguity that might dull the edge of American heroism. The Department of Defense's Entertainment Media Office, housed in Los Angeles, still reviews hundreds of scripts each year. Its influence is often invisible but unmistakable: a phrase softened, a mission reframed, an error omitted in the name of operational security—or national myth.

For the services, this is marketing. For the studios, it is realism. For the public, it blurs the line between memory and message. The result is not falsehood but curated truth—heroism without context, sacrifice without policy, war without politics. Audiences come away believing what the camera permits them to see: courage untainted, violence redemptive, victory inevitable.

Every generation inherits these films and mistakes them for history. They become the collective memory—the cinematic scripture of the Republic. From *Midway* to *Lone Survivor,* from *The Longest Day* to *American Sniper,* **Hollywood's lens** has mirrored the nation's shifting conscience yet always returned to the same frame: that **valor justifies the mission, even when the mission is unclear.**

This partnership has consequences. It insulates the public from the true costs of war and allows policymakers to wage it without shared sacrifice. When the spectacle of heroism replaces the dialogue of accountability, the state gains not just a narrative but an audience conditioned to applaud it. Propaganda has evolved—not through censorship, but through collaboration.

Lesson: The alliance between **Hollywood and the Pentagon** has always been about **control**—of **image**, of **memory**, of **moral tone**. Cinema became the new parade ground, and the reel became the recruiting poster. In every era, the camera has done what policy could not: turn **conflict into entertainment**, and **entertainment into belief**.

PART II

VIETNAM AND THE FRACTURED NATION

6

INDOCHINA: VIETNAM AND THE FRACTURED NATION

The Vietnam War did not erupt out of nowhere. Its roots reached deep into the 1920s, when European empires still stretched across the Pacific and the Near East. The French in Indochina, the British in Malaya and Burma, the Dutch in Indonesia — all ruled through the language of civilization while practicing the mechanics of exploitation. Railways and plantations were built not for freedom, but for profit. Colonial borders were drawn by surveyors who never saw the mountains or rivers they divided. Those lines, artificial and absolute, became the fault lines of the next century.

Out of this system grew two contradictions that would shape modern Asia. The first was the awakening of national identity — local movements that saw independence not as rebellion but as the fulfillment of their own history. The second was resentment: decades of humiliation under foreign rule disguised as progress. France justified its empire through what it called the *mission civilisatrice* — the claim that colonial rule existed to civilize, educate, and modernize subject peoples. In practice, that doctrine delivered forced labor on plantations and infrastructure projects, food extraction that fueled famine, cultural erasure, and imprisonment or violence for anyone who questioned authority. Resistance was labeled criminal rather than political, allowing domination to be framed as discipline. The seeds of Ho Chi Minh's revolution were sown in those prisons and plantations long before Marx or Mao became scripture.

World War II cracked those empires but did not erase them. When Japan's occupation collapsed in 1945, power across Asia became contested ground. The Allied victors — Britain, France, the United States, and the Soviet Union — imagined that new international institutions could stabilize the chaos. Out of that hope, and fear, came the United Nations, a fragile coalition of victors still wearing wartime habits, meant to keep order where empires had failed. It was the UN that oversaw Korea's postwar elections, partition, and fragile democracy after Japan's withdrawal.

For a moment, it seemed to work. When North Korea invaded the South in 1950, the United Nations authorized what it called a "police action." It was war by another name, fought largely by American troops under a multinational flag. The result was ambiguous but survivable — a stalemate that saved half a nation and appeared to validate the model of intervention. **Korea became proof that Western leadership, backed by technology and unity, could check aggression and preserve democracy.**

The lesson was **dangerously oversimplified**. What

worked on the peninsula of **Korea — bounded by sea, reinforced by global consensus** — could not be replicated in the jungles of Indochina. The same playbook that seemed to contain communism in Korea would become a catastrophe in Vietnam.

By then, the United States had assumed a new identity: the world's custodian. **The Truman Doctrine** pledged resistance to communism anywhere it appeared. The Marshall Plan had rebuilt Europe and vindicated the belief that America's resources and moral clarity could fix what war had broken. From Washington, to London, to Paris — postwar leaders saw themselves as heirs to the a new world one led by America, with men shaped by Depression, world war, and victory. They were disciplined, confident, and convinced that their sacrifices had earned them the right to remake the world in their image.

But that faith carried a blindness. The same generation that had defeated fascism also learned to equate dissent with disloyalty and instability with evil. They had seen appeasement fail once and vowed never to let it happen again. Their courage hardened into certainty; their experience became dogma. It was that generation — the sons and protégés of those who fought at Normandy and Iwo Jima — who would send others' sons into Vietnam. They carried forward their fathers' playbook: contain the enemy, trust the system, believe in victory. They could not imagine that their war might end differently.

When France attempted to reclaim Indochina after Japan's surrender, Washington framed it not as colonialism reborn but as the next front in the struggle against communism.

To abandon the French seemed unthinkable; to question the cause seemed unpatriotic. The **United States financed eighty percent of France's war costs.** The more the French fought for empire, the more America convinced itself it was fighting for freedom.

When **Dien Bien Phu** fell in **1954**, the illusion collapsed. **France departed humiliated**, but America refused to learn the lesson. Instead, it assumed command. The Geneva Accords divided Vietnam at the 17th Parallel, promising national elections that never came. Washington feared a communist victory more than it trusted democracy. Containment replaced self-determination as strategy.

From that point, every decision was made in the name of prevention — stopping what might happen elsewhere. **The Domino Theory turned every village in Southeast Asia into a symbolic Berlin or Budapest. Laos, Cambodia, and Vietnam became chess pieces in a game played thousands of miles away by men who still believed in the righteousness of their fathers' wars.**

By the early 1960s, advisors had become Soldiers, and Soldiers had become an army. Helicopters replaced rhetoric; body counts replaced progress reports. What began as a Cold War containment mission metastasized into a quagmire of ideology, fear, and inertia. **By 1968, more than 543,000 Americans were deployed in Southeast Asia** — fighting a revolution they could not define, for a victory they could not describe, in a country they did not understand.

Lesson: Vietnam was not born from chaos but from continuity — from inherited faith in power, order, and moral mission. The same generation that built the postwar world also built the trap that would consume its sons.

The Architects of Attrition

They brought the blueprints of Normandy to the paddies of the Mekong. The same slide rules that measured bomb tonnage over Tokyo now calculated kill ratios in **Quảng Trị.** Their confidence had been hardened by victory, their uniforms pressed by memory. They had defeated fascism, rebuilt Europe, and believed — deeply — that American willpower, technology, and moral clarity could solve any problem. But in the jungles of Vietnam, the equations no longer worked.

The **architects of the war were not naïve men**. They were the best-educated, most decorated officers and policymakers of their generation — veterans of a righteous war who believed they had mastered the mechanics of victory. They carried the lessons of World War II like sacred scripture: that planning, firepower, and production could overcome any enemy; those good intentions redeemed terrible means; that the end of evil justified whatever it took to win.

John F. Kennedy, the young PT-109 hero, embodied the promise of the postwar elite. He surrounded himself with other veterans — the "best and brightest" — to prove that intellect and vigor could contain communism just as firepower had defeated fascism. In their hands, war became a policy instrument, a manageable enterprise of advisors, helicopters, and measured escalation.

Robert S. McNamara, a former bomber statistician, trusted numbers more than nuance. As Secretary of Defense, he reduced war to data: sorties flown, villages pacified, bodies counted. Each week's briefing felt like a ledger of progress, but the math was sterile. No formula could quantify faith, fear, or national will. His rational systems measured motion, not meaning.

General William Westmoreland, schooled in artillery and attrition, believed firepower would break the enemy's back. He chased a crossover point – the moment when communist losses would exceed their ability to replace them – never seeing that Hanoi's calculus was moral, not mathematical. In his reports, success was a number; in the paddies, it was a rumor.

Behind them stood **General Maxwell Taylor**, paratrooper of Sicily and Normandy, who championed "flexible response." He saw Vietnam as the proving ground for limited war – a laboratory where American strength could be applied in controlled doses. Yet in practice, the dose kept increasing, and the patient kept dying.

They were not monsters. They were men of discipline, faith, and extraordinary competence – the Greatest Generation's heirs to empire. But they had learned how to end wars, not how to avoid them. They mistook the clarity of 1945 for a universal law of history. Their tragedy was not ignorance but misapplied mastery.

And perhaps the **cruelest irony – they had seen everything before**. They were the witnesses. The cities burned from the air. The camps liberated in silence. The bodies stacked in neat, efficient rows. They were the men who had watched the worst of humanity and swore it would never happen again — yet somehow, under their watch, it did.

Kennedy, who had seen men burned alive in the Pacific, now approved the use of napalm in Southeast Asia. McNamara, who once calculated bombing efficiency over Japan, now counted bodies in Vietnam. Westmoreland, who had witnessed Europe's firestorms, now presided over free-fire zones and strategic hamlets that emptied entire villages. Taylor, who parachuted into Normandy to liberate Europe, now defended policies that displaced peasants and poisoned paddies in the name of progress.

They were not blind; they were accustomed. In their memories, atrocity had become routine, sanitized by experience and stripped of shock. They had learned that moral horror could coexist with bureaucratic order — and they built systems to manage it rather than prevent it. The firebombing of Tokyo became the template for Rolling Thunder. The logistical miracle of D-Day became the supply chain of attrition. The ledger of tonnage, sorties, and losses became the new scripture of modern war.

By the time the photographs of My Lai surfaced, they had already seen worse — just not in color, and not on the evening news. They knew the look of incinerated children; they had seen it before. They had watched moral shock turn into mission drift, and then into policy. They understood the paradox that atrocity, when repeated, becomes procedure. The horror was not that they didn't know. It was that they did — and they kept going. Because to stop would mean admitting that everything they had built since 1945 was founded on a lie: that victory through firepower could create peace, that moral authority could survive mechanized killing, that a **good man could order bad things** and remain unscarred.

Vietnam became the mirror of their youth — a reflection of the same faith in industry, discipline, and control. But this time, there was no liberation, no parade, no moral certainty — only statistics and silence. By 1968, the body count had replaced the moral compass. The same nation that once liberated Europe now counted corpses to justify strategy. The veterans of Omaha Beach had become administrators of attrition.

When it ended, not with victory but with silence, they stood bewildered before the mirror of their own creation. They had built another monument — this time not of marble but of metrics — and beneath it lay the ghosts of two generations: those who led, and those they sent.

They were the sons of victory who became the fathers of ambiguity — and the war they built was the bridge between triumph and doubt.

The Draft and the Exodus

For families across America, the war was not an abstract policy but a lottery with life-and-death stakes. The draft became its central symbol. A low lottery number could send a boy to the jungle; a deferment could save him. Wealth and privilege often made the difference. Sons of lawyers and politicians found college deferments, medical excuses, or slots in the National Guard. Sons of farmers, factory workers, and single mothers were sent to fight.

In my father's family, the lottery felt personal even when the numbers never came. His eldest brother, Steve, born in 1950, earned college deferments and spent those years in classrooms instead of jungles. The middle brother, Mike, born in 1952, drew a high number and watched friends vanish into basic training while his own draft card gathered dust. My father, born July 18, 1954, registered because every young man still had to — but by the time his name could have been drawn, the last lottery had already been held. The draft ended one step before his generation. They were the standby sons, carrying cards that would never be called — inheriting a war they were prepared to fight but never asked to.

In our family, that quiet relief and lingering guilt still divide the kitchen table — between those who waited, those who served, and those who simply came too late.

Some refused outright. Between **40,000 and 150,000 Americans fled to Canada**. Tens of thousands more sought refuge in Sweden or the UK. Around **210,000 men were formally accused of draft evasion, with thousands imprisoned.**

My own family lived this dilemma. My grandfather Wade Hart had fought on Okinawa in World War II. He was proud of his service. He loved his country. But he swore his sons would not go to Vietnam. If the draft came, he was willing to relocate the entire family out of the country either to Canada or elsewhere. His reasoning was not cowardice — it was scars. He had seen the carnage of war up close and refused to sacrifice his children to another jungle.

For families like ours, Vietnam was not just foreign policy. It was survival, principle, and betrayal all tangled together.

The Child Conundrum — From Vietnam to the GWOT

Perhaps no dilemma captures the moral impossibility—and the haunting connection between Vietnam and the Global War on Terror—better than what Soldiers have long experienced and without a name a battlefield question and probability: *the child conundrum.*

A patrol approaches a hut. Inside could be a weapons cache. Or a trap. Or a child. For thirty days, every visit to the village has meant ambush or sniper fire. The Soldier must choose: act first and risk killing an innocent or hesitate and risk dying—or watching a buddy die.

In Vietnam, the unspoken rule was simple: *throw the grenade*. Survive. It was a logic born not of cruelty but of exhaustion, fear, and the mathematics of chance. A wrong decision meant a folded flag. That first time was the last time a soldier risked himself—or his friend—on hesitation. Nearly all engagements would end in violence either way.

After **1973**, when the **draft ended** and the **All-Volunteer Force emerged**, American doctrine changed. Positive identification (PID), increasingly restrictive Rules of Engagement

(ROE), and the burden of restraint fell squarely on the individual Soldier. Yet the moral weight of killing did not change. The decision still lived in the same heartbeat between doubt and death.

What a society demands of its fighters—kill quickly or die carefully—reveals as much about its culture as its strategy. Do we condemn the Soldier who fires and kills a child; or send them to prison? Do we scold the one who shoots at an empty hut? Do we mourn the one who dies because he hesitated? These are not hypothetical questions. They are the moral arithmetic imposed on young men barely more than boys, and carried home as unspoken confessions.

Vietnam forced these questions into the open under uniquely corrosive conditions. Soldiers were drafted as individuals, often entering units with little shared history or long-term cohesion. In that environment, authority fractured. Leaders who attempted to enforce stricter discipline or moral restraint sometimes faced lethal backlash. Fragging—Soldiers killing their own officers with grenades or ambush—became a grim symptom of a force under unbearable strain, where trust collapsed and survival eclipsed obedience.

Unlike the mass-unit rotations of earlier wars, Vietnam's system of individual replacement and rapid air transport created a new kind of dissonance. A Soldier could be in the killing fields of the Mekong Delta on a Wednesday and watching a drive-in movie stateside by Friday night. Forty-eight hours separated combat from suburbia. There was no decompression, no ritual of return, no preparation for crossing that psychological border. One moment he was scanning tree lines;

the next he was sitting at a kitchen table where no one knew what to ask—and he did not know what could be said.

The pattern repeated decades later, in different terrain and under different acronyms. In Iraq and Afghanistan, the child conundrum returned—not in huts, but in alleys and doorways, in convoys and checkpoints. We had technology our fathers never imagined: drones, optics, data links. Yet for all our precision, the moral equation was unchanged. We would rather die confirmed than live condemned.

For modern Soldiers, hesitation became both virtue and liability. Doctrine demanded PID before engagement—a safeguard intended to preserve legitimacy, but one that often required men and women to absorb risk until the instant of death. Better to come home in a flag-draped coffin than in handcuffs. Better to be remembered as honorable than to live accused of atrocity by a society that no longer understood what collateral damage even meant.

And so the pendulum swung from moral numbness to moral paralysis. The Vietnam generation was scarred by excess; the GWOT generation was scarred by restraint. In both cases, the burden of judgment fell on the same people—those with boots in the dust, forced to decide in seconds what the nation would debate for years.

On a dry, hot day, I found myself conducting a dismounted sweep through the village of Wahgez, in Ghazni Province. Intelligence reported a possible enemy cache. We moved deliberately. In that village, coalition units had been engaged by the Taliban almost every day for the previous three weeks. We absorbed all of the risk—dismounted, slow, mine-detection deliberate, checking for buried IEDs as I walked near point.

We swept south until we were positioned to cover potential enemy movement. The village had been active moments earlier, but suddenly the people disappeared. It went deathly quiet... people went inside... it felt exactly like a movie of impending danger.

I came to a fixed position near the end of an alley between qalats (qalats being a general name for a middle eastern small 1 or 2 story family or business structures generally made of stone or dried mud brick). About fifteen feet in front of me set into the qalat wall, was a closed window with shutters, and a door. I fixed my attention on the door. Suddenly, it began to open. I raised my M-4 Carbine, rotated the selector from safe to fire, and prepared for the worst.

A boy jumped out.

The look on his face—seen through my optic—I will never forget. He froze, staring down my rifle. I hesitated, confirmed PID – noncombatant, rotated the selector from fire back to safe, lowered my weapon, waved the child back inside, and only then realized I had started breathing again.

I am grateful for my training. That day, no cache was found. The Taliban did not engage us—once. It was the first and last time that village did not erupt under contact.

I carry that child's life in my hands.

I know Soldiers who were not afforded that chance. One Soldier I knew described a raid as part of a professional discussion. His squad came under fire from an adolescent boy hiding under a bed—whether or not the child was connected to Saddam Hussein's former regime I make no comment. The squad responded with a fragmentation grenade the firing ceased from the room and they continued clearing the target.

Another Soldier—a woman, not in a combat-arms branch—found herself clearing a house. In a bathroom stood a boy holding an AK-47 Rifle. As she opened the door, the child began to raise the rifle. He lacked training. A shot rang out immediately from her M-16 Rifle.

War finds children—directly and indirectly—even now.

The technology that carried us home erased the distance between war and peace, but it offered nothing to bridge the space between memory and silence. The flight home was only the first step in America's longest war—the one fought in the minds of those who returned.

Lesson: Vietnam taught America that without clarity of purpose and honesty from leadership, national will collapses. The Global War on Terror taught that restraint without understanding wounds just as deeply as excess.

Understanding can wound as deeply as aggression. Both revealed that atrocities are rarely accidents—they are outcomes of policy and distance. Each generation has faced the same reckoning: what do we demand of a Soldier—survival at any cost, or restraint at the risk of their life?

During an operation in Ghazni Province, the issues of PID, rules of engagement, and collateral damage asserted themselves once again.

Giro District was the hottest area in Ghazni at the time—a divisional-level priority. A month after experiencing the chaos and combat in Khōgyani, I understood how quickly a situation could move from stable to unstable, and from bad to catastrophic. Because of the unique nature of this operation, I will limit certain details, but the facts remain.

From our outpost, using persistent surveillance cameras—which demonstrates just how close we were, at most a few kilometers from the engagement—I observed and visually confirmed, along with other officers in the operations center, the movement of approximately 75 to 150 individuals. They appeared to be women and children leaving the village. Almost immediately after their departure, our troops began taking fire.

Over the next 24 hours, due to the rules of engagement, we were only able to engage the enemy using helicopters and Polish 98mm mortars. We had F-16s, F-15s, and at one point an A-10 on station. None were permitted to engage the village. Fast movers were prohibited from striking targets within the village or within 1,000 meters of it due to concerns about civilian casualties... yes even though we observed what appeared to be all the women and children leaving.

The Taliban timed our air assets precisely. US AH-64 Apache helicopters from FOB Sharana and Polish MI-24 Hind gunships from FOB Ghazni would arrive, and enemy fire would cease. As soon as the helicopters departed, the firing resumed.

Over the course of the operation and the days that followed, coalition forces suffered significant losses. We incurred **15 coalition casualties wounded**. Including Afghan contractors, total wounded, killed, and missing ranged between **35 and 40**. Five of our Tactical Vehicles of various types were destroyed. If Afghan contractor vehicles—semi-trucks and large jingle trucks—are included, **roughly 30 vehicles** were **lost.** Two vehicles were destroyed on the first day when Taliban fighters threw grenades into them after the vehicles made a wrong turn inside the village.

We did engage targets within the village when permitted. Some helicopter strikes successfully destroyed enemy machine-gun positions, and we eliminated a mortar team.

The mission was only partially completed, but I succeeded in moving my contractors, engineers, and Soldiers through the gauntlet. I requested to remain on site while the unit conducted retrofit operations; that request was denied by the deputy commander of Task Force White Eagle. In hindsight, that decision likely saved my life.

I was extracted by helicopter—sent specifically for me—from COP Giro to FOB Ghazni. I took a cold shower (I can count on one hand the number of hot showers I had in Afghanistan) and finally slept. The next day, a Polish captain—the head of supply and logistics—came to my tent to inform me that the commander at COP Giro had called. He said it was a good thing I had been ordered out: a mortar round had destroyed the cot I had been sleeping on—and would have slept on again.

Ultimately, we accomplished the primary mission I had been ordered to complete at COP Giro, but at great cost. The base was later transitioned to U.S. forces the following summer, allowing the Polish Army to reduce its footprint and begin its planned withdrawal from Ghazni Province and Afghanistan.

Had this been Vietnam, the outcome in Whagez and Giro

would have been very different. We would have destroyed the qalats. We would not have risked walking point with mine detectors. We would have created distance between ourselves and any potential combatants or noncombatants and eliminated all suspected cache locations.

In Giro, our aircraft would have struck targets we already had eyes on. We knew civilians had left the village; tactically, it was a clearer environment. But that did not happen. The village remained standing. Machine-gun teams fired. IEDs detonated. The enemy withdrew, regrouped, and waited.

They survived mostly.

We survived mostly.

The war simply continued.

The Child Conundrum – From Vietnam to Today

The dilemma never ended. It only changed uniforms.

The following is a condensed illustration of a rather well-known incident – one Hollywood has told and truth has come out over a decade later. In a condensed version of events 2005, a four-man Navy SEAL reconnaissance team was compromised in the mountains of Kunar Province, Afghanistan. Their mission—Operation *Red Wings*—was to locate a high value target (HVT) a Taliban commander responsible for killing dozens of Marines. While watching over a remote valley, the team encountered unarmed goat herder, a teenage boy. They detained him, they debated their fate, and made a decision that would haunt every after-action review and movie script that followed: they released him.

Hours later, a dozen at most Taliban fighters ascended the ridge. **Three of the four** SEALs were killed. The lone survivor, Marcus Luttrell, was rescued days later by an Afghan villager who risked his own live to protect him. The mission became both legend and controversy—a reminder that mercy can cost lives, and that the difference between righteousness and ruin can be a single act of compassion.

Hollywood turned *Lone Survivor* into a hymn of endurance. What it could not capture was the internal calculus that every Soldier knows too well—the choice between killing an innocent and risking your brothers. The SEALs followed the laws of war, but the law could not protect them from consequence. They chose restraint, and they died for it. That truth is not cinematic; it is tragic, human, and endlessly recurring.

Nearly twenty years later, a different story surfaced—buried in classified reports and quiet briefings until investigative journalists uncovered it. A Navy SEAL team, operating covertly off the coast of North Korea, was compromised during an insertion . Civilians on a fishing vessel had witnessed their presence. The SEALs, fearing exposure that could ignite an international crisis, opened fire. The civilians died. The details remain partially redacted, but the decision echoes through every combat zone before and after: *to kill for silence, or to die for mercy.*

The Navy handled it differently this time. There were no press tours or patriotic soundtracks, no blockbuster redemption. The incident was acknowledged internally, investigated quietly, and absorbed into the doctrine of realism that governs special operations—ugly, necessary, and known only to those who bear its weight.

That difference matters. In **Afghanistan, compassion led to annihilation**. In **North Korea, caution led to atrocity**. In both, the men involved will live forever with the same question that haunted their fathers in Vietnam: ***what was right in the moment no one else will ever see?***

The child conundrum did not die in the jungle; it followed us into the mountains, the deserts, and the dark water. Every generation of warriors meets it again—in doorways, on ridgelines, or through rifle scopes. The decision is never clean. The rules are never enough.

These servicemen live with those moments long after the cameras stop rolling. The burden is not only what they did, but what they chose not to do. For them, the conundrum is not theoretical—it is the echo that wakes them at night, the question that has no answer, and the silence their families inherit.

Lesson: The child conundrum lives on. It is the crossroads of conscience and survival, where humanity and duty collide. Every generation faces it, and every nation that sends its sons and daughters to war must live with what they decide when no one is watching.

The Winter Soldier and the Hidden Files

In January 1971, in a Detroit hotel ballroom, more than a hundred veterans gathered for what they called the Winter Soldier Investigation. They described what they had seen and done:

burning villages with Zippo lighters, executing prisoners, raping civilians, counting the dead indiscriminately as "enemy kills." Their words shocked many, enraged others. The government dismissed them as liars or radicals.

But the truth was far darker than even most Americans suspected.

In the wake of the My Lai massacre's exposure in 1969, the Pentagon quietly created a task force called the **Vietnam War Crimes Working Group (VWCWG).** Its mission: review and track allegations of atrocities committed by U.S. forces. For years, Army investigators compiled reports, producing over **9,000 pages of documents**.

By the early 1970s, those files **documented 320 substantiated incidents** of atrocities — massacres of civilians, rapes, torture by electric shocks and beatings, mutilation and desecration of bodies. **Another 500 cases were judged "plausible but unverified."** And this figure **did not** even **include My Lai**, which was investigated separately.

The files were classified. Buried. Forgotten. It wasn't until the mid-1990s that the documents were declassified and placed in the National Archives. Journalists like Deborah Nelson and Nick Turse uncovered them. Nelson's 2006 Los Angeles Times investigation and Turse's book *Kill Anything That Moves* revealed what the government had long denied: **atrocities were not isolated.** They were systemic, woven into the very **policies of the war.**

Free-fire zones, body count quotas, and search-and-destroy missions all but guaranteed civilian deaths. Soldiers were rewarded for kills, not for protection. Dehumanizing language turned every Vietnamese into a "gook," every corpse into a statistic. The Winter Soldiers had been right. They spoke the truth years before their government admitted it.

The veterans who testified at Winter Soldier carried not only guilt but language yet to be invented. In 1972, psychiatrists who worked alongside them—among them Dr. Chaim Shatan, Robert Jay Lifton, and Sarah Haley—began calling it **Post-Vietnam Syndrome (PVS).** It described what could not yet be diagnosed: the persistence of war in memory and behavior, the feeling that part of Vietnam had followed them home. It was not an illness so much as a haunting, a conflict between conscience and survival that no discharge could erase. Years later the term would evolve into **Post-Traumatic Stress Disorder (PTSD)** in the medical lexicon, but the original phrase was more honest. It acknowledged that the wound was not only psychological but cultural—a fracture between the veteran and the nation that had sent him.

Politicians would later twist that vocabulary into Vietnam Syndrome, **turning trauma into policy and shame into strategy**. One phrase sought healing; the other sought forgetting. For those who had served, both were accurate in their own way.

Lesson: Truth is never comfortable, and conscience is never convenient. The Winter Soldiers exposed not only atrocities but the system that required them. The buried files proved what silence had long protected — that the machinery of war runs on obedience until someone refuses to lie. **Vietnam's true wound was not defeat abroad but denial at home, and the cost of that denial was faith itself.**

Collapse of National Will

At home, the war dragged on while trust in leadership eroded. The Gulf of Tonkin incident, used to justify escalation, was later revealed to have been exaggerated. Pentagon officials massaged body counts; presidents promised progress even as coffins multiplied. The rhetoric of "peace with honor" masked a reality of attrition without purpose.

By **1975**, when helicopters lifted off the embassy roof in Saigon, **58,000 Americans were dead. Millions of Vietnamese, Cambodians, and Laotians had perished.** The war had consumed a generation and fractured the nation's faith in itself.

The same country that had once rebuilt Europe now struggled to comprehend what it had destroyed in Asia—and in its own soul. For America, the war ended with silence and evacuation. For South Vietnam, it ended in fire.

I watched **Ghazni** collapse to the **Taliban in 2017**—six years after we had fought, bled, and died there. It was not the first time a city had fallen, but it was the first time I watched memory itself collapse. The same outposts, the same ridgelines, the same districts we had rebuilt with our hands and held with our dead were gone in a week. Not conquered—abandoned.

When **Kabul** fell in **2021**, the images were déjà vu: helicopters circling an embassy, panicked crowds at a perimeter, promises dissolving in real time. The old footage of Saigon found its mirror on new screens. To most Americans, it was history repeating; to those who had fought in Afghanistan, it was history echoing—louder this time because we knew the sound.

The Vietnam veterans understood. They reached out quietly, not with speeches or advice but with recognition. They had felt this before: the hollow quiet after a mission without victory, the sting of pride turning to shame, the long flight home to a country already moving on. They called us their desert sons and daughters. We called them our jungle parents.

They knew what it meant to watch the ground you fought for burn. They had lived through the helicopters over Saigon and the silence that followed. They carried the same guilt—the same questions that never find answers. When **Abbey Gate** exploded outside Kabul's airport, **killing thirteen service members and nearly two hundred Afghan civilians, they didn't need an explanation.** They had seen that look before—in their own mirrors half a century ago.

The names changed—Saigon became Kabul, Hue became Ghazni—but the feeling was the same: the ache of unfinished work, the disbelief that sacrifice could dissolve so quickly, the quiet knowledge that honor does not depend on outcome.

The Vietnam veterans adopted us not because we asked, but because they recognized the weight we carried. They had walked through the same aftermath, and they understood that wars do not end when the last plane leaves the runway—they end when the memory of those who served is finally heard.

Lesson: History repeats its endings more faithfully than its beginnings. Every generation of warriors learns that the hardest part of war is not fighting it—it's living long enough to watch it fall apart.

7

THE LAST COMMANDER

When history closed in on South Vietnam, one man still believed it could be held. **Major General Lê Minh Đảo,** commander of the **18th ARVN Division**, stood at the edge of collapse and refused to surrender to inevitability. In April 1975, as North Vietnamese divisions rolled down Highway 1 toward Saigon, Đảo's division took its position at **Xuân Lộc** – a small city that had suddenly become the hinge of an entire war.

His Soldiers were outnumbered **ten to one**. They were fighting on fumes, short of ammunition and air support, surrounded by artillery, tanks, and certainty. Yet they held. For nearly two weeks the 18th Division fought like a dying man's heartbeat – slow, deliberate, unwilling to stop. Under Đảo's command they turned every street into a trench, every building into a redoubt. He moved among them without theatrics, calm and unshaken, the kind of commander who led with quiet conviction instead of speeches. He told his men that the capital still depended on them. They believed him because they needed to. The battle of **Xuân Lộc did not save South Vietnam**, but it delayed its death. **It bought time – time**

for families to flee, for the last helicopters to find rooftops, for the world to watch something that looked like honor amid collapse. When Saigon finally fell, Đảo refused evacuation. He **stayed with his troops**, **surrendered with dignity**, and disappeared into the system that swallowed the defeated.

He spent seventeen years in "re-education" camps — years of beatings, starvation, and labor under guards who wanted him broken but never found the key. By the time he was **released in 1992**, the flag he had fought for was a relic sold in flea markets. He came to the United States like so many others — stripped of rank, past, and purpose — another refugee in a country that had promised not to abandon him and then did.

In Connecticut he found work managing a restaurant. **The man who had commanded the last organized defense of Saigon** now took orders and **cleared tables** for people who never guessed what those hands had done, what orders they had once given, what silence he carried. He **died** there **in 2020, largely unnoticed** outside the Vietnamese-American community — **a general without a country, a Soldier whose last campaign was survival.**

History will remember him, if it remembers him at all, as the commander who bought South Vietnam its final days. But those who know the story understand something deeper: that courage does not always save nations, and dignity does not guarantee remembrance. Lê Minh Đảo fought not for politics but for his men, for the principle that duty does not end when hope does. He kept faith when the world looked away.

He was, in the end, a man of immense grace in erasure — a Soldier left to live among the indifferent, serving strangers in the country that had once called him ally. History rarely honors those who lose beautifully. But sometimes the truest measure of a Soldier is the quiet endurance of one who stood his ground until there was nothing left to defend but honor itself.

Lesson: Vietnam was not just a military defeat. It was a moral and political collapse. It proved **that democracies cannot sustain war without clear purpose, honest leadership, and shared sacrifice.** And it showed that atrocities are not "bad apples" — they are what happens when policy rewards body counts over humanity.

8

WAR IN FILM

Few wars have been filmed, debated, and re-imagined as much as Vietnam. Each director, each production, has tried to capture a conflict that for America was as much psychological and cultural as it was military. The result is not one definitive movie but a mosaic of perspectives — symbolic, literal, traumatic, and redemptive — that together trace the American experience of Vietnam.

Apocalypse Now (1979) is remembered less for accuracy than for symbolism. Francis Ford Coppola transformed Joseph Conrad's Heart of Darkness into a Vietnam epic, using the river journey into Cambodia as a descent into moral chaos. It is surreal and exaggerated, yet in that exaggeration it captures the madness, futility, and disorientation many veterans recall.

Platoon (1986), Oliver Stone's semi-autobiographical account, swung the pendulum back to realism. Stone himself served in Vietnam, and the muddy foxholes, endless patrols, and moral struggle between Sergeants Elias and Barnes were drawn from lived experience. For many veterans, this film came closest to the "grunt's war" – the mud, the jungle, the firefights, and the moments when right and wrong blurred in the smoke.

Full Metal Jacket (1987) split the war into two acts: boot camp and battle. R. Lee Ermey's performance as the drill instructor is legendary, but it is more than entertainment. Stanley Kubrick showed how training dehumanized recruits, stripping individuality, then dropped them into Hue's urban combat where confusion and cynicism reigned. It is a symbolic portrait of how a generation of young men were reshaped – and scarred – by war.

The chose a different path, following steelworkers from Pennsylvania before, during, and after Vietnam. Its infamous "Russian roulette" sequence has been criticized for invention, yet its broader truth is undeniable: Vietnam came home with the Soldiers, fracturing friendships and hollowing out families. The trauma of captivity, the alienation of return, and the slow unraveling of small-town America were as real as the jungles themselves.

We Were Soldiers (2002) revisited the war's beginning rather than its collapse, portraying the 1965 Battle of Ia Drang – the first major engagement between U.S. forces and the North Vietnamese Army. Based on Lt. Gen. Hal Moore and journalist Joe Galloway's account, it captured the moment America's confidence met the reality of modern war. Its power lay in showing both the discipline and the despair of men realizing that courage alone could not control chaos. Unlike the detached cynicism of later Vietnam films, *We Were Soldiers* honored valor without glamorizing victory. It revealed how devotion, leadership, and sacrifice could coexist with futility — a reminder that even the most righteous intentions cannot redeem a war already slipping beyond reason.

And then there is *Born on the Fourth of July* (1989). More than any other film, it bridged combat and aftermath. Based on Ron Kovic's autobiography, it follows a Marine paralyzed in combat who becomes an anti-war activist. In doing so, it captured not only the war but the homecoming, not only the firefight but the protest. Tom Cruise's performance traced the journey from patriotic idealism to betrayal, disillusionment, and ultimately advocacy. The film revealed America's divided soul: the pride of service, the cost of war, and the bitterness of returning to a country that no longer knew what to make of its veterans.

Each of these films, in its own way, told a true story — whether literal or symbolic. Each director took both acclaim and criticism, yet together they form the cinematic testimony of Vietnam. They do not agree, but neither did America. And in that discord, they may be truest of all, for Vietnam was not one story but many: courage and chaos, duty and despair, pride and protest. Perhaps no other film captured the full transition — from battlefield to bedroom, from parade to protest — better than *Born on the Fourth of July*.

Forrest Gump and Project 100,000

Most viewers see *Forrest Gump* (1994) as a story of innocence and destiny. They miss the darker echo: Forrest is, in many ways, a cinematic stand-in for the thousands swept up by Secretary of Defense **Robert McNamara's Project 100,000**.

Launched in 1966, the program lowered entrance standards to feed Vietnam's insatiable demand for manpower. one hundred thousand men — many poor, rural, or from minority communities — were recruited despite failing aptitude tests they were as they said at the time medically "**retards**". They were promised training, skills, and opportunity. In reality, most were sent **straight into combat**, where **cas-ualty rates were two to three times higher** than average.

Forrest's unquestioning service, his obedience without com-prehension, his miraculous survival — all mask a grim truth. For every "Gump," countless real men went into the jungle unable to read a map, confused by orders shouted under fire, dead before their stories could be told. Historians later called them McNamara's Morons, a phrase as cruel as it is revealing.

The film softens Vietnam into caricature: hippies reduced to noise, wounded veterans to props of tragedy, Forrest's innocence to redemption. Real veterans came home to hostility, poverty, and silence. Lieutenant Dan's bitterness was closer to the truth than Forrest's shrimp-boat salvation.

Project 100,000: The Bureaucracy of Triage

If boot camp was triage for the body, then Project 100,000 was triage for the soul. McNamara's promise to "broaden oppor-tunity" cloaked a bureaucratic arithmetic: more bodies for a war already bleeding its best.

The men who arrived under his numbers were processed like replacement parts — trained by drill sergeants who already knew the odds. Many instructors privately called the program morale triage. They followed orders but understood what it meant to send the unprepared into a war that no one was winning. Discipline became mercy: to shout, to strike, to drill endlessly — because hesitation would kill these boys faster than the enemy could.

Statistics later confirmed what the cadre already knew. The so-called New Standards Men **died** in Vietnam at **nearly double the rate of other Soldiers**. They came home in disproportionate numbers in coffins or wheelchairs, their names missing from the policies that sent them. McNamara's experiment revealed a darker truth about American efficiency: when war becomes a data problem, people become expendable solutions.

The system that trained them had no malice; it had only mission. That was the tragedy. As capitalism rewards output without empathy, the war machine rewarded obedience without question. These recruits were not shaped into citizens; they were rendered into instruments. Their humanity was triaged before they ever reached the field.

Lesson: Project 100,000 and *Forrest Gump* remind us how war exploits the least powerful. Heroism may inspire, but policy decides who pays the price — and too often, it is those with the least voice.

PART III

AMERICA'S NEW WARS

9

1973 AND THE ALL-VOLUNTEER FORCE

On July 1, 1973, America ended the draft. For the first time since World War II, no young man would be compelled by law to wear the uniform. The Vietnam War had broken the social contract; the draft was seen as unjust, disproportionately sending the poor and minorities to die while the wealthy secured deferments. President Nixon, guided by the Gates Commission, promised a different path: a professional, all-volunteer military.

The early years were rough. Recruiting slumped, drugs and indiscipline plagued the ranks, and morale sagged. Project 100,000 — Robert McNamara's disastrous scheme to draft the "substandard" into service during Vietnam — had left a bitter legacy of wasted lives, men sent to die with no preparation but a quota to fill. By the late 1970s, many wondered if a volunteer army could even survive.

Slowly, it did more than survive — **it transformed**. Competitive pay, the GI Bill, and improved training began to attract recruits who *wanted* to be there. Military families — the sons and daughters of veterans — increasingly formed the backbone of the force. By the **1980s, service had become self-selecting** and, in many cases, hereditary. What emerged was a pipeline: Junior ROTC in high schools, ROTC on college campuses, and the service academies. Enlistment clustered in particular regions and families, reinforcing a distinct military subculture increasingly separate from the broader nation. Even popular culture reflected this shift, with figures like **John Travolta** appearing in early Army advertising campaigns that framed service as purposeful, professional, and aspirational. Like travel sports leagues, this pipeline honed its players. Just as a child in elite soccer learns year-round discipline, a teenager raised in a military town is steeped in service long before raising their hand. By the 1990s, the U.S. fielded a force smaller than in the draft era, but leaner, more skilled, and more professional than any in its history.

The promise of an all-volunteer force was freedom from coercion. The **cost was a widening civil–military gap**. Without a draft, fewer families bore the burden. The military became excellent — but also isolated.

10

DESERT STORM - PRECISION AND ILLUSION

In January 1991, the United States and its coalition partners unleashed a storm over the Persian Gulf. For the first time, the **all-volunteer force** created in 1973 was tested in a large-scale war. It was not the ragged citizen army of Vietnam but a professionalized military pipeline — hardened by years of selective recruitment, honed in training centers, and equipped with technologies that had seemed unimaginable only a generation before.

Operation Desert Storm lasted only six weeks. From the opening air campaign to the lightning-fast **"hundred-hour ground war,"** the results were stunning. American precision-guided munitions struck targets with uncanny accuracy. Abrams tanks swept across the desert with overwhelming speed, smashing Iraq's armored divisions almost before they knew they were under attack. Fewer than **300 Americans were killed** — a number so low compared to Vietnam that it seemed almost unbelievable.

For the public, the war unfolded live on **CNN.** Cameras showed green-tinted footage of bombs dropping down chimneys, night skies lit with tracers, and Patriot missiles arcing upward to intercept Iraqi Scuds. War had become a broadcast spectacle — clean, efficient, and strangely bloodless on the screen. Gone were the chaotic images of Vietnam: the confusion of jungle firefights, the wounded carried on stretchers, the body bags. Desert Storm looked, at least to American eyes, like a technological triumph. (The Death highway was shown, reminiscent of the images of the Failise pocket, and thousands of dead horses and German equipment were decimated after being encircled by allied forces in the breakout of Normandy in the summer of 1944. President H.W. Bush himself a member of the greatest generation; had been a Naval Aviator, a bomber pilot and saw combat in the Pacific, himself even being shot down on a combat mission.

For many, it was vindication. The all-volunteer force had worked. After years of doubt about whether a professional military could match the mobilized citizen armies of the past, here was proof: discipline, competence, and overwhelming victory. The shadow of Vietnam seemed banished in a single dazzling campaign. The very idea of a draft now appeared absurd — why disrupt the lives of millions when a small, professional pipeline could deliver results so quickly?

Yet beneath the celebration lay an illusion. Desert Storm's brevity and low cost created a dangerous precedent: the belief that America could wage war **without broad sacrifice.** The burden would fall on the professional caste of the military, while the rest of society watched on television, applauding from the sidelines. Casualty figures, not strategic outcomes, became the measure of success.

The generals spoke of a **"revolution in military affairs."** Precision-guided weapons, real-time satellite intelligence, and digital communications seemed to promise a new kind of war — one where technology replaced the ancient brutalities of attrition and bloodshed. But what this revolution truly offered was **insulation.** The pipeline of **the all-volunteer force would absorb the risks and hardships, sparing the broader public from the pains of sacrifice.** War could be fought far away, fast and efficient, as if detached from the nation itself.

The illusion was seductive. Desert Storm suggested that technology had solved the riddle of war. That professionalism, satellites, and smart bombs had erased the fog and friction that had humbled armies for centuries. But history rarely cooperates with illusions. In the decade that followed, America would test this belief again — in the Balkans, in Somalia, and, after September 11, in wars that would prove far less quick, far less clean, and far more costly than the spectacle of 1991 had led the nation to believe.

11

SHADOWS BETWEEN WARS

The parades of Desert Storm faded quickly. Yellow ribbons were taken down, Soldiers returned to bases, and America slid into the 1990s with a sense of unrivaled power. The Soviet Union had collapsed, the Berlin Wall was rubble, and the U.S. military had just crushed Saddam Hussein's army in a matter of weeks. To most Americans, history itself seemed to have turned a corner. Technology and professionalism had tamed war. The draft was a relic. The "Vietnam Syndrome" was declared dead.

But war has a way of shifting its ground. The decade between the victory parades of 1991 and the horror of September 11, 2001, was not the peaceful interlude many imagined. It was instead a period filled with warnings — bloody episodes that revealed America's new vulnerabilities. They were real, deadly, and deeply important. Yet in the moment they were underplayed, treated as distant tragedies, quickly folded into the background noise of prosperity. Only later would their significance become undeniable, shaping the road to the War on Terror.

Mogadishu, 1993

In Somalia, famine had drawn the U.S. into a humanitarian mission. Food convoys were guarded by Soldiers, and Marines patrolled dusty streets. But soon America found itself entangled in clan warfare, fighting not hunger but warlords. On October 3, 1993, in Mogadishu, a mission to capture lieutenants of Mohamed Farrah Aidid spiraled into disaster.

Two Black Hawk helicopters fell from the sky, struck by rocket-propelled grenades. On the ground, Rangers and Delta Force operators fought block by block, outnumbered and surrounded. Eighteen Americans were killed, dozens wounded. Hundreds of Somalis also died, many of them civilians caught in the crossfire.

The most haunting images came after the shooting stopped: the body of an American Soldier dragged through Mogadishu's streets, broadcast on television screens back home. The battle shocked the military, but the public treated it as an aberration. Somalia was far away, difficult to pronounce, harder to place on a map. President Clinton ordered U.S. forces withdrawn soon after. The lesson was clear to those in uniform — that lightly armed militias could humble the world's superpower — but for the nation at large, it passed almost unnoticed.

The Embassy Bombings, 1998

Five years later, in August 1998, near-simultaneous truck

bombs exploded outside U.S. embassies in Nairobi, Kenya, and Dar es Salaam, Tanzania. The blasts killed over 200 people, including 12 Americans, and injured thousands more. It was one of the deadliest terrorist attacks against U.S. targets in history. Behind it was a name still unfamiliar to most Americans: **al-Qaeda.**

President Clinton ordered cruise missile strikes against suspected terrorist camps in Afghanistan and a pharmaceutical plant in Sudan. Critics mocked the action as a "distraction" from domestic scandal. Few grasped that these bombings marked a new kind of war — one not fought with tanks and armies, but with car bombs and cells hidden in shadows.

The USS Cole, 2000

On October 12, 2000, the destroyer USS Cole pulled into Aden, Yemen, for refueling. As sailors prepared lines, a small boat sidled up, its crew smiling and waving. In the next moment, the boat exploded, tearing a massive hole in the ship's hull. Seventeen American sailors were killed instantly.

Investigators quickly linked the attack to al-Qaeda, but again, the news faded. The country was consumed by the contested 2000 presidential election, debates over recounts and ballots in Florida. The deaths of those sailors barely registered beyond military circles. Yet for those watching closely, the Cole was a warning flare. Terrorists had struck directly at a U.S. warship, in broad daylight, and gotten away.

Other Warnings

There were more. The **Khobar Towers bombing** in 1996 killed 19 U.S. Airmen in Saudi Arabia. Smaller plots were uncovered and foiled. Intelligence agencies whispered about Osama bin Laden, who had declared jihad against America. But outside of government and military communities, these events were treated as peripheral.

The economy was booming, the internet was transforming daily life, and war seemed far away. America had come to believe in the Desert Storm illusion: that conflict could be quick, clean, professional, and insulated from ordinary citizens. These bloody warnings did not fit the script. And so, for most, they barely existed.

Underplayed but Defining

In hindsight, the pattern is stark. Mogadishu showed that even irregular fighters could humble American forces. The embassy bombings revealed the global reach of al-Qaeda. The Cole attack proved U.S. warships were vulnerable. Each event exposed weaknesses — in strategy, in intelligence, in imagination.

Yet in the 1990s, they were treated as footnotes. There were no national parades of mourning, no sweeping mobilizations, no great debates about war and peace. The professional military absorbed the blows while civilian society remained largely untouched. The pipeline of the all-volunteer force insulated the public from sacrifice, just as Desert Storm had promised it would.

But the enemies of the United States had been watching. They saw a nation drunk on its own triumph, distracted by prosperity, and unwilling to fully reckon with the new kind of war emerging from the shadows.

And when September 11, 2001, came — when hijacked planes turned into missiles and the towers fell — it was not out of nowhere. It was the culmination of a decade of warnings ignored, the dark harvest of battles and bombings that had slipped beneath the radar. Desert Storm had promised clean, quick victory. The 1990s had whispered otherwise. Only later would Americans realize those whispers had been the opening notes of the War on Terror.

PART IV

MODERN COSTS

12

GWOT - NATIONAL WILL AND THE PIPELINE'S BURDEN

The Surge of Unity

On September 11, 2001, everything changed again. The attacks on New York and Washington shattered illusions of safety and united the nation in fury and grief. For a brief moment, America experienced the same solidarity it had known after Pearl Harbor. Flags flew from porches. Blood banks overflowed. Congress authorized war almost unanimously.

The all-volunteer force surged into Afghanistan, and two years later into Iraq. At first, the professionalism of the pipeline shone. Units deployed quickly, executed with precision, and overwhelmed adversaries. The contrast to Vietnam was stark: no draft protests, no chaotic conscription. For most Americans, life went on uninterrupted. Shopping, work, entertainment — war was something fought by others, somewhere else.

The life of **Pat Tillman** crystallized this convergence of sports culture and military ethos. An NFL star with a multimillion-dollar contract, Tillman walked away after 9/11 to enlist in the Army Rangers. His discipline, forged on the football field, found its echo in the regiment. His death in Afghanistan in 2004 — and the cover-up that followed — turned him into both a symbol of sacrifice and a cautionary tale about how even heroism can be manipulated. He was proof of the pipeline: how a culture of discipline and sacrifice could produce warriors.

Tillman's story resonated because it reassured the country that sacrifice was still voluntary, noble, and evenly shared. It suggested that the right people were stepping forward, that courage and character were sufficient answers to national trauma. In that moment, the distinction between choice and assignment was easy to ignore.

But the very clarity of that narrative concealed something more structural. The All-Volunteer Force did not distribute risk broadly; it concentrated it. What appeared as individual choice was already shaped by position — by geography, by class, by access, by familiarity with service as inheritance rather than exception. The system did not compel participation, but it did not ask everyone equally.

The pipeline made this distinction invisible. Recruitment, training, assignment, and deployment worked together to absorb national will without spreading national cost. War could be authorized collectively while its consequences settled predictably on a narrow segment of society. Less than one percent of the population wore the uniform. The rest bore witness.

This was not a failure of patriotism. It was a success of design. The nation could remain unified precisely because most citizens did not have to alter their lives in response to war. The burden fell where it always had — on those born closest to it.

Only later would the consequences of that concentration become visible.

The Weight of the Burden

But the very success of the system concealed its strain. With no draft to spread the burden, the same communities, the same families, carried it tour after tour. Fathers and sons deployed back-to-back; mothers left infants to serve again. Less than one percent of the population wore the uniform, while the other ninety-nine watched on television.

From inside the force, the pattern was visible even at the lowest levels. As a junior Officer in Afghanistan, serving in unbrevetted position, I was not shaping policy or directing strategy. I was watching how the war moved. Units rotated on schedules that felt prewritten. The same formations returned through the same valleys. The same names reappeared on rosters. Vietnam had taught the institution how to fight without mobilizing the nation; Afghanistan showed that lesson refined. The machine did not improvise. It cycled.

War arrived less as chaos than as procedure. Briefings reduced terrain, people, and risk into timelines and slides. Intelligence came already processed, already framed. Decisions moved downward quickly; responsibility followed orders; consequence settled elsewhere. It was efficient. That was the danger.

By the late 2000s, the cracks showed. PTSD and moral injury rose sharply. Suicides climbed. Families fractured under repeated deployments. And yet the wars went on — easier to sustain precisely because the burden was so narrowly carried.

The professional force had given America excellence. But it had also created distance. War had become both everywhere and nowhere — fought by a caste of warriors, endured by their families, but largely invisible to the nation they served. The All-Volunteer Force did not eliminate sacrifice. It routinized it. And because the system worked, it kept going.

Khōgyani, 2011 — The Lesson About Death and Fear

We told ourselves it was different. New century, new weapons, new doctrine. But in Khōgyani, the truth felt ancient. The Taliban fought with the same patience and cruelty the Japanese once used on my grandfather's generation. They learned every fold in the ground, every approach to the outpost. They watched, waited, and struck when we were certain the valley was quiet. The night belonged to them.

They came close — always closer than you thought they could. The attacks weren't random; they were rehearsed. Feints and lures, radio silence before contact, fighters slipping through irrigation cuts like shadows. When they attacked, it wasn't chaos. It was deliberate, personal, and meant to unnerve. It reminded me of the stories of Okinawa and

Guadalcanal, of men who crawled through mud and darkness to test the courage of whoever stood guard.

Fear works the same way no matter the language. It finds the gaps — in wire, in vigilance, in the mind. Once it gets in, it doesn't leave. The enemy knows that. They always have.

When the district center fell in 2010, it wasn't just a tactical loss; it was a message. When we came to rebuild it the next summer, we were building on top of that message. Every bag of cement, every section of Hesco was a statement that we could outlast fear. But fear doesn't care about fortifications. It seeps in anyway.

We had all the technology in the world, but on nights when the valley went still, the difference between us and the Marines in 1942 disappeared. You could feel it — that same animal understanding that death was close, that the enemy was watching, that courage was just another word for endurance.

The Echo of Elah

If *Born on the Fourth of July* was the cinematic testimony of Vietnam, then In the Valley of Elah became the quiet lament of the Global War on Terror. Where Ron Kovic's story screamed of betrayal and alienation, Hank Deerfield's search in Elah whispers — a father uncovering the truth of what war had done to his son, only to find that the battle did not end in Baghdad. It followed him home to the barracks, to the backroads, to the morgue.

For veterans of Iraq and Afghanistan, this film struck a

nerve. It did not dazzle with firefights or chopper blades thumping across desert skies. Instead, it showed the silence of return — young Soldiers unable to speak of what they had seen, unable to reintegrate, turning inward toward violence, drugs, or despair. It showed a family trying to make sense of wounds that carried no Purple Heart, of scars that left no clear line between heroism and homicide.

The potency of *In the Valley of Elah* lies in its honesty: the war followed them home. It lived in the nightmares, in the short tempers, in the alienation that made a father realize his son had been changed in ways no uniform or medal could redeem. For GWOT veterans, the film was not a tale of distant history but a mirror — one that forced audiences to reckon with the truth that these wars were not just fought overseas. They came back with every service member and rippled through every kitchen table.

And in that, the story connects generations. The quiet of the "Greatest Generation," the anger of Vietnam, the disillusionment of the Gulf and Iraq — each war left its imprint not only on those who fought but on those who waited. In the Valley of Elah makes that inheritance plain. It says out loud what many families already know: war is not finished when the last shot is fired. It endures in memory, in behavior, in addiction, in silence.

These scars connect fathers to sons, mothers to daughters, veterans of Tarawa to Fallujah, from the jungles of Vietnam to the deserts of Tikrit. The uniforms change, the landscapes change, but the burden carried home remains hauntingly the same. That is why *In the Valley of Elah* is so potent: because it dares to show that the **true battlefield** of the American veteran has always been both **abroad and at home** – and that the **cost** of war is always, inevitably, a **family** burden to bear.

Lesson: The GWOT proved both the strength and the weakness of the all-volunteer pipeline. It produced unmatched warriors, but at the cost of deepening the civil–military divide and making endless war politically easier, because so few bore its weight.

13

THE RULES OF ENGAGEMENT (ROE)

The concept of ROE was born in combat. Soldiers are taught three principles: positive identification (PID), proportionality, and escalation of force (EOF). ROE is not about hesitation; it is about discipline. By design, it restrains Soldiers so that war does not collapse into massacre, Clarity is its strength.

In Iraq and Afghanistan, I lived under this standard. The most common, most honest justification for action was simple: **"I feared for my life, and the lives of my Soldiers.**" That phrase, grounded in ROE and backed by command authority, saved lives and kept violence disciplined. When those rules are clear, they give the Soldier both moral and legal cover to act decisively without descending into chaos. When they are vague, fear replaces focus, and hesitation replaces judgment.

The doctrine exists for a reason. **Every trigger pull** carries moral and strategic consequence. ROE keeps the rifle connected to the conscience, ensuring that the power to kill never outruns the responsibility to decide. It is the architecture of restraint — the invisible wall between discipline and disaster.

I helped write force-protection policy for the Illinois National Guard in 2016, ensuring our Soldiers understood when to act and when not to. The standard was clear, unwavering, and absolute. Had we ever failed to provide that clarity — had our troops faced a threat without guidance or authority — the result would have been confusion, panic, and blood.

Lesson: ROE matter not only on battlefields but anywhere the state wields force. Soldiers know it. Police Officers know it. When rules are clear, they channel violence into order. When they are absent or confused, chaos fills the void.

The Breach — January 6 and the Failure of Command

On January 6, 2021, the U.S. Capitol was stormed. Officers stood on marble steps unsure when — or if — they could use force. Riot shields and helmets had been withheld. Requests for reinforcements stalled, tangled in bureaucracy and fear of political optics. Publicly elected officials cowered in chambers while mobs shattered windows, beat officers, and threatened to hang the Vice President of the United States.

Clarity was absent. The Capitol Police and National Guard operated in a fog of politics rather than a chain of command. When to engage? How much force was permitted? Who had the authority to say "enough"? Questions multiplied while rioters advanced. Officers were left to improvise, restrained not by doctrine but by paralysis.

From my own experience — over 15 years of Army training,

deployments in combat zones, and as the author of Illinois National Guard policy on force protection —I comfortably can say without hesitation: there was dereliction of duty at the command level. The men and women on those steps were not cowards. They were denied the Doctrine, equipment, and authority to act all existed. Had a suicide bomber been in that crowd — a scenario explicitly drilled into force-protection plans and mass-casualty training for large public events — the result could have been mass slaughter. The idea that defenders of the nation's legislature stood armed yet unable to escalate or contain, awaiting permission to meaningfully exercise force while the building was breached, is indefensible; leadership failure was negligent and culpable on all sides.

The irony was cruel. The very doctrines forged to regulate violence overseas — doctrines that allowed me to protect my Soldiers in Mosul, Tikrit, and Kandahar — were not applied to the defense of the Republic's own seat of government. Had those officers been given the same clarity of ROE we demanded in combat, the breach might have been repelled, lives preserved, and democracy spared the spectacle of chaos inside its own halls.

Lesson: Discipline is not the enemy of freedom; it is its defense. When leaders abandon clarity, they abandon those who stand the line for them. On January 6, chaos won — not because America lacked defenders, but because those defenders were left without rules.

A Nation Polarized, a Veteran's Reality

The pardons of January 6th Rioters did not heal division — they widened it. For some, they were mercy; for others, they were betrayal. The effect is that the rift in American society has grown deeper, harder, more intractable. One side now believes that loyalty supersedes law; the other fears that legal protections no longer defend allegiance to principle but protect power.

But for veterans, the pardons revealed a deeper truth we already knew: society had failed many of its children before the uniform ever called. The Capitol insurrection was not merely an assault — it was a public revelation of an avoidable tragedy. These individuals were not born radicals; they were molded in neglect, abandoned by systems of disillusionment.

The true tragedy was not ten thousand arrests followed by ten thousand pardons. The catastrophe was that ten thousand officers did not escalate and protect the Capitol from violent attack. They were negligent and derelict, and history judges this too gently. It has laid the foundation for uglier second- and third-order effects. By the time violence erupted on the Capitol steps, the damage had already been done.

We asked our "blue line" siblings — our brothers and sisters in uniform and in force — to hold the line, to protect democracy. They did so at terrible cost: physical injury, broken morale, emotional scars. But they succeeded, in a narrow sense. The 2021 elections were transferred for the first time in American history under such circumstances — a fragile testament that democracy, though shaken, held.

Yet new alarms are now echoing. The unprecedented meeting between the Commander in Chief and General Hegseth in Quantico declaring war on US Cities and soil should be a clarion call. It was more than optics; it was a message. The person entrusted with civilian command instructed military leadership to wage war on U.S. cities? — an instruction unthinkable in any stable constitutional democracy. Such direction in public view mocks the wall separating armed forces from domestic politics. It demands that we ask: what lessons have we learned? What lessons have we forgotten?

If we cannot answer those questions — if we cannot hold true to the principle that disciplined force must always bow to law — then the polarization, chaos, and future violence we fear might become the new normal.

The Honored and the Fallen

In August 2025, the White House reversed an earlier decision and granted military funeral honors to Ashli Babbitt, the Air Force veteran who died of wounds received while attempting to breach a restricted hallway inside the U.S. Capitol on January 6, 2021. The decision followed a review ordered by the new administration and a letter from Air Force Under Secretary Matthew Lohmeier authorizing full ceremonial recognition: flag presentation, rifle volley, and the playing of Taps. It was an act both symbolic and seismic — a government reinterpreting the morality of its own insurrection.

The announcement reignited a national argument that still

divides the country. Supporters viewed the honors as a gesture of forgiveness, a recognition of her prior service and sacrifice. Critics saw it as a distortion — the sanctification of rebellion under the flag meant to prevent it. How, they asked, **can a person who died storming the seat of democracy be honored under the same standard as those who died defending it?** Can loyalty to a cause excuse defiance of the Constitution sworn to be protected? And if treason is too strong a word, what word remains for violence against one's own republic?

For veterans, the debate was not theoretical. Military honors are more than ritual; they are moral currency. Every folded flag, every note of Taps, is the nation's promise that sacrifice made in uniform aligned with its values. When those honors are extended to someone who turned that uniform inward, the question becomes existential: **What does the oath mean if its boundaries are negotiable?** As a Soldier, I know that restraint is what separates duty from chaos. On January 6, that restraint failed. Four years later, the act of granting honors to one of its participants reopened that wound — not only the physical breach of the Capitol but the moral breach in America's understanding of service. Is patriotism an emotion, a principle, or simply the willingness to fight under any flag? The answers have become partisan, but the questions are timeless.

At its core, the debate over Ashli Babbitt's funeral honors is not about one woman, or even one day. It is about ownership of memory — who gets to define courage, loyalty, and betrayal when all three wear the same uniform. Some call her a martyr; others call her a warning. Both views reveal a truth we have long avoided: that citizens and Soldiers alike can lose their way when outrage replaces oath.

In the military, we are taught that honors are earned through service, not sentiment. In a nation increasingly divided over what "service" means, that distinction is fading. Granting Babbitt military honors did not reconcile the country — it exposed its fracture. It showed that the line between hero and heretic is drawn not by the dead, but by the living, and that every generation redraws it to fit its own reflection.

Lesson: Discipline is not the enemy of freedom; it is its defense. When leaders rewrite the meaning of sacrifice for convenience, they risk unbinding the very oaths that hold the Republic together.

14

THE FAMILY BURDEN

Every war follows Soldiers home. It follows in silence at the dinner table, in the burn of whiskey at the VFW, in children raised by parents who are present in body but far away in spirit.

The "Greatest Generation" often kept quiet, their trauma unspoken. Vietnam veterans spoke out more, but many still drowned their pain in alcohol or isolation; or their own independent rap groups, or VFW canteens. GWOT veterans came home to social media tributes but few neighbors who understood. The civil–military gap meant their wars were often invisible, their wounds harder to share.

Children grow up in these households' carrying echoes: sometimes pride, sometimes fear, sometimes patterns of anger or silence they cannot name. Families inherit war, even if they never wear the uniform; often combinations.

Even in the fiercest campaigns of history, the aftershocks of war have extended into the veteran's home front — in spirit and in the body. Alcohol misuse is not a modern invention. It has shadowed military communities from Tarawa to Tikrit.

In World War II, the heavy stress of combat, long separations, and trauma contributed to high rates of alcohol misuse among returning veterans. Some historical sources suggest that more than half of WWII veterans admitted to acts of alcohol abuse at some point in their lives — not necessarily alcoholism by medical definition, but misuse tied to coping with the memories of war.

In subsequent wars — Korea, Vietnam, the Gulf, Iraq, and Afghanistan — the pattern persisted: combat trauma, PTSD, readjustment stress, and gaps in support created fertile ground for substance misuse, with alcohol often being the ubiquitous option. While mortality records rarely listed "alcohol use disorder" as the explicit cause of death, many veterans who died by suicide, liver disease, or accidents likely had alcohol as a contributing factor.

Modern studies confirm that the burden is real. Today, more than **40% of U.S. veterans** have a lifetime history of Alcohol Use Disorder. Between **2012 and 2018** alone, **2,421 veteran deaths** were recorded in alcohol-involved overdoses (868 were alcohol-only, the rest combined with other substances). Other research estimates **21,861 alcohol-attributable deaths** in veteran populations when stratifying by demographics and risk factors.

Thus, while the clarity of data increases in modern times, the underlying trend is unchanged — some veterans do not die by bullets or bombs but by the slow, cumulative damage of alcohol. The silent casualties of war include not just the visible wounds but the hidden torment of addiction, which, as we see today, claims lives long after the fighting ends. And families bear that burden too: in broken relationships, in financial instability, in children learning silence instead of laughter.

Lesson: The question is not whether to tell children about war. It is how. To sanitize is to lie. To burden them with horror is unfair. To tell the truth with love is the only path that honors both the dead and the living.

15

TARAWA TO FALLUJAH - THE BOTTLE AND BARREL

On paper, the United States lost **1,000 Marines in the three days** it took to capture **Tarawa** in November 1943. The numbers are stark, and the graves at the Punchbowl and Arlington confirm the cost. But those numbers do not capture the Marines who lived — the men who carried nightmares home, turned to the bottle in silence, and sometimes ended their own lives long after the parades ended. Suicide has always been part of war's unfinished ledger.

Tarawa: Silent Wounds (PTSD) of the Greatest Generation

World War II veterans rarely spoke of "**trauma.**" In the medical literature, it was called "**combat fatigue**" or "**shell shock**." For many who fought at Tarawa, Guadalcanal, or Normandy, their greatest struggle was not the Japanese or

Germans but their own memories. Studies of the **WWII cohort** show increased rates of **depression** and **suicide** in the decades after the war, though the cultural code of silence often **disguised** it as **heart disease, alcoholism, or "accidents."**

Vietnam: Naming the Invisible

By the 1970s, the stigma of silence cracked. Soldiers returning from Vietnam confronted not only flashbacks and hypervigilance but also a hostile homecoming. Vietnam Veterans Syndrome VVS Congressional testimony – including the 1971 Winter Soldier hearings and John Kerry's Senate testimony – forced the nation to confront the moral injuries of war. The Department of Veterans Affairs began documenting post-traumatic stress disorder in Vietnam veterans, linking PTSD with higher rates of substance abuse and suicide. Veterans like Philip Caputo (A Rumor of War) and Tim O'Brien (If I Die in a Combat Zone) gave words to what earlier generations could not say: war followed you home.

GWOT: A War Without End

In Iraq and Afghanistan, the pattern intensified. Unlike WWII or Vietnam, the All-Volunteer Force deployed again and again. Some Soldiers rotated through Tikrit, Mosul, and Kandahar four or five times. The Department of Defense reports that more U.S. servicemembers have died by suicide than in combat in the post-9/11 era. A 2021 report from Brown University's Costs of War project estimates more than **30,000 post-9/11 service members and veterans have taken their lives** – a number dwarfing **battlefield death** counting a little over **7 thousand** as of 2026.

The battlefields of Fallujah, Ghazni, may be quiet, but for many veterans the war persists nightly. Unlike Tarawa, where silence concealed, or Vietnam, where anger spilled outward, the GWOT generation posts online pleas, farewell notes, or fragmented memories before adding their names to the daily toll – **17 to 22 veterans lost to suicide every day in the United States**. Men and women devastated by a war they fought on behalf of a **country** they answered for **people who just don't understand nor care.**

The Generational Thread

Tarawa. Vietnam. Marjah. Different wars, different enemies, but a single through-line: the human mind is not immune to combat. From the widow who never understood her husband's quiet withdrawal after WWII, to the Vietnam veteran who wrestled with shame in the 1980s, to the Iraq veteran who died by suicide after multiple deployments – these stories are not aberrations. They are evidence of a generational echo.

What We Owe Them

The United States is adept at building memorials for those killed in action. It struggles to acknowledge those killed by memory. Suicide is too often dismissed as a private tragedy. In reality, it is a national responsibility, a deferred cost of every war since 1776. The Marine who falls in Okinawa, the Soldier who dies by overdose in 1978, the staff sergeant who hangs himself in a barracks outside Tikrit — all are casualties of combat.

If Tarawa taught courage and Tikrit demanded endurance, the lesson that echoes between them is this: to honor the fallen, we must see those who fall at home. The hidden war must be brought into the national memory.

PART V

RECKONING AND LESSONS

16

WHAT WAR REMINDS US

After all the stories — Guadalcanal, Normandy, the Holocaust, Vietnam, 1973, GWOT, January 6th — the question remains: what lessons do the horrors of war teach us?

1. **That comfort breeds forgetting.** Every generation relearns lessons neglected in peace.
2. **That technology magnifies morality.** From the Maxim gun to Hiroshima to drones, invention outpaces ethics.
3. **That national will is fragile.** It hardens in crisis, fractures in ambiguity, and erodes in endlessness.
4. **That civilians always pay.** In Caen, in Hiroshima, in My Lai, in Kyiv — the innocent are targets, collateral, or shields.
5. **That silence is deadly.** Atrocities thrive when survivors do not speak, or when society refuses to listen.
6. **That families inherit war.** The ghosts do not stop at discharge. They walk through kitchens, classrooms, playgrounds.

7. **That truth-telling is a form of patriotism.** Winter Soldiers, archives, memoirs — these keep us honest.

The deepest lesson is humility: that war always costs more than leaders predict and always stains deeper than societies admit.

Death Becomes 8 Bits (Digital)

In 2022, Russian tanks rolled toward Kyiv. Mothers dragged children through snow toward the Polish border; men queued for rifles older than they were; cities burned beneath the crosshairs of modern optics. During the Winter Olympics, television cut from Ukrainian athletes to a composed Vladimir Putin in his luxury box — weeks from ordering the largest land invasion in Europe since 1945.

The war felt both distant and familiar. Distant, because Americans witnessed it through screens instead of draft notices. Familiar, because its patterns were old: a superpower underestimating resistance, civilians shouldering as much as Soldiers, propaganda warring with truth.

What remains unseen is what matters most — the invisible inheritance. Trauma etched into children. Families scattered like refugees across generations. We see burned-out tanks but not the young men who will one day wake in darkness hearing engines that are no longer there.

McNamara's Line — The First Digital War

Half a century earlier During Vietnam, Secretary of Defense Robert McNamara believed machines could rationalize chaos. His "Electronic Barrier," later called McNamara's Line, dropped thousands of seismic and acoustic sensors along the Ho Chi Minh Trail. Signals flowed through IBM computers in Thailand, each blip a promise that data could replace judgment.

It was brilliant in concept and catastrophic in practice. Water buffalo triggered bombers; monsoon rains spoofed readings; billions bought confidence without clarity. Yet the greatest failure was moral: officers began trusting algorithms over instinct. Coordinates replaced conscience.

That line was the first digital frontier — where the distance between decision and death could be measured in bits. It taught the Pentagon a dangerous lesson: that war could be managed from afar, and that abstraction was a form of comfort.

AI at the Edge of the Battlefield

Today that comfort has become doctrine. In Ukraine, artificial intelligence is no longer theoretical; it is operational. Drones that once scouted now hunt. Algorithms scan hours of video in seconds, flagging targets before a human can blink. Some systems already recommend — or authorize — lethal fire.

"Death Becomes 8 Bits" is digital and literal. A bit is binary: 0 or 1. Yes or no. In modern war, death can be decided by a drone correlating shapes through software — pattern matched or rejected, target confirmed or dismissed. When control is lost or time collapses, the system answers the question on its own: kill or do not kill. In that moment, death is no longer judged. It is computed. Unlike the Soldier who hesitates, machines feel nothing. They do not measure fear, mercy, or regret. They do not carry moral injury home to their families. They calculate, and they execute. The algorithm is a perfect Soldier — obedient, tireless, and without soul.

If Vietnam was the first experiment in digital war, Ukraine is its graduation. McNamara's dream — a battlefield of sensors and circuits — has arrived, stripped of hesitation and conscience. For the first time, machines are not merely observing war but participating in it.

This is not progress; it is amnesia. Each upgrade erases a lesson learned in blood. Each new interface pushes the human heart one click further from the trigger. Technology promises precision but delivers detachment. It multiplies efficiency while dividing accountability.

And the infection is spreading. Predictive algorithms guide policing. Surveillance AI patrols borders and cities. The same logic that targets a convoy in Donetsk can profile a citizen in Chicago. Lines between war and law enforcement, between Soldier and civilian, blur with each iteration of code.

An algorithm does not know the Bill of Rights. It does not understand proportionality, restraint, or the Constitution we swore to defend. It understands input and output. If we allow it to decide who to watch, detain, or kill, then the republic will not collapse from violence but from delegation — from turning our most sacred moral decisions into mathematics.

Modern war is lived in both images and silences. What is seen is destruction; what is unseen is inheritance. Every generation receives its own version of Guadalcanal — whether in mud, in jungle, in desert, or in code.

In the digital age, that gap widens. When death is reduced to a binary decision — a 0 or a 1, yes or no — distance grows faster than accountability. Machines do not remember. Algorithms do not inherit silence. The burden still returns to us.

WAR'S ETERNAL LESSON

A nation at war rarely behaves as a collection of individuals. It behaves as a mob —certain of its righteousness, insulated by distance, buoyed by shared purpose. Judgment becomes collective. Responsibility diffuses. Moral weight is suspended. The crowd moves together, convinced that necessity itself is justification.

But the crowd does not form in a vacuum.

Economic position is assigned before agency ever begins. Birth, class, geography, and access determine who is most exposed to risk long before choice enters the story. Societies that deny this reality convert inequality into moral judgment: success becomes virtue, failure becomes fault. From that judgment grows anger. From shared anger comes national will.

National will makes war possible. It supplies legitimacy, urgency, and moral cover. Violence is framed as duty. Sacrifice becomes honor. Responsibility is collectivized. Decisions belong to "us." Outcomes are owned by "the nation." The crowd feels righteous because no one bears the weight alone.

But war does not end where the crowd thinks it does.

When the fighting stops, the crowd disperses. The banners come down. Attention moves on.

Responsibility—long deferred—collapses back onto individuals, disproportionately onto those who carried out the violence in the first place. Veterans are left holding memories that were once shared abstractions. What had been framed as necessary becomes personal. What had been celebrated becomes unspeakable.

This is not an accident. It is a pattern.

It is in this fracture—between collective action and solitary memory—that moral injury, survivor's guilt, and long-term psychological harm take root. The same society that collectivized decision-making individualizes consequence, offering ceremony instead of accountability, gratitude instead of reckoning.

Sacrifice therefore concentrates predictably at the margins, while the crowd moves on unburdened.

The Logic, Distilled — With Historical Overlay

1. **Economic position** is assigned before agency.
   Colonial empires (pre-1914), the Great Depression (1930s), the All-Volunteer Force (post-1973).
   Who carries risk is decided long before war begins.

2. **Denial of that fact produces moral judgment**.
   World War I patriotism, WWII total mobilization, post-9/11 rhetoric.
   Structural inequality is reframed as personal virtue or failure.

3. **Moral judgment converts into crowd anger.**
   Yellow journalism (1898), anti-Bolshevik fear (1919), Cold War paranoia, post-9/11 rage.
   Complexity collapses into blame.

4. **Crowd anger is mobilized as national will.**
   1917, 1941, 1964, 2001.
   Political leaders give anger direction and call it resolve.

5. **National will enables war.**
   World War I, World War II, Vietnam, the Global War on Terror.
   Violence becomes authorized, normalized, and necessary.

6. **Responsibility then collapses back onto individual veterans.**
   Civil War GAR era (1870s–1890s), Bonus Army (1932), Vietnam veterans (1970s), GWOT veterans (2000s–present).
   Those who executed policy are left to carry its cost.

7. **The crowd disperses before the bill arrives.**
   Post-1865 reunion, post-1918 isolationism, post-1975 Vietnam

silence, post-2021 Afghanistan withdrawal.
Attention moves on while consequences remain.

8. **War allows a nation to act like a crowd, but forces its veterans to remember as individuals.**
   Guadalcanal patrols, Normandy survivors, Vietnam platoon leaders, drone operators.
   Collective action becomes solitary memory.

9. **In this fracture, moral injury and long-term psychological harm take root.**
   Alcoholism and suicide among Civil War veterans, shell shock after WWI, PTSD after Vietnam and GWOT.
   The damage is not only physical.

10. **Collective decision-making** becomes individualized consequence, masked by ceremony.
    Parades, medals, "thank you for your service," flyovers, memorial days.
    Gratitude replaces accountability.

11. **Sacrifice** concentrates at the margins; the crowd moves on unburdened.
    Less than one percent fight; fewer still return unchanged.
    The cost is carried by a shrinking few.

What is remembered as national resolve is lived as private reckoning.

Acknowledgments:

No book is written alone. This one began in fragments—notes from deployments, conversations at kitchen tables, and quiet moments beside headstones—and became whole only through the patience of those who believed it mattered.

I owe my first debt to the Soldiers, Marines, Airmen, and Sailors who trusted me with their stories. Some spoke in detail; others said only a sentence and let the silence finish it. Every one of them shaped these pages.

To my family—especially my parents and sister and immediate family—thank you for carrying the weight of service in your own ways. My father's generation taught me the cost of waiting, my grandfather's the cost of fighting, and my mother's the cost of both.

To friends and mentors who challenged every paragraph and asked harder questions than I did—your insistence on truth over comfort made this book stronger.

To the historians, archivists, and librarians who preserve memory when it is easiest to forget—your quiet discipline is the foundation of every honest history.

And finally, to the reader: for choosing to engage rather than turn away. If these stories stir unease, good. It means you are listening. Memory is not meant to be comfortable; it is meant to keep us human.

Major (Retired) Michael P. Hart

About the Author:

Michael P. Hart, Major (Retired), MBA, GC-HRM, is a retired U.S. Army Officer who bridges leadership, war, and memory. A veteran of more than a decade of service—including overseas deployment and years spent leading soldiers—Hart brings both the discipline of military service and a servant's perspective to his writing.

Hart's work is shaped by firsthand experience with the systems that send people to war—and the consequences that follow long after conflicts end. His writing explores the intersection of history, leadership, memory, and moral responsibility, with particular attention to the human cost that lives behind official records and statistics.

He holds a Bachelor of Science in Law Enforcement and Justice Administration, a Master of Business Administration, and a Graduate Certificate in Human Resource Management. A student of military history, culture, and policy, Hart is drawn to the stories that exist between formal documentation—where duty, loss, and meaning are often negotiated rather than recorded.

Hart writes across history, leadership, and moral inquiry, seeking not only to preserve the record of conflict but to examine how societies remember, forget, and pass those experiences forward. When not researching or writing, he is an outdoorsman and traveler who finds restoration in quiet places and with a guitar in hand.

Commonly Used Acronyms and Abbreviations

AAR — After Action Report (Post-mission review; Ch. 12)

AI — Artificial Intelligence (Automated decision/analysis; Ch. 16)

AMA — American Medical Association (Volunteer physicians in Vietnam; Ch. 4)

AO — Area of Operations (Assigned battlespace; Ch. 12)

AP — Associated Press (Global news wire; Ch. 1)

ARVN — Army of the Republic of Vietnam (South Vietnamese Army; Ch. 6–7)

AWOL — Absent Without Leave (Unauthorized absence from duty; Ch. 13)

BCT — Brigade Combat Team (Modular Army brigade formation; Ch. 12)

BDA — Battle Damage Assessment (Evaluation of strike effects; Ch. 10)

BLUF — Bottom Line Up Front (Staff communication style; Ch. 12)

CALL — Center for Army Lessons Learned (Institutional learning arm; Ch. 11–12)

CAS — Close Air Support (Aircraft supporting ground troops; Ch. 8, 12)

CBRN — Chemical, Biological, Radiological, Nuclear (WMD hazard category; Ch. 5)

CIA — Central Intelligence Agency (Foreign intelligence agency; Ch. 6, 11)

CJCS — Chairman of the Joint Chiefs of Staff (Top uniformed advisor; Ch. 9)

CJCSI — Chairman's Instruction (High-level DoD guidance; Ch. 13)

CNN — Cable News Network ("CNN effect" on Desert Storm; Ch. 10)

COIN — Counterinsurgency (Doctrine to defeat insurgency; Ch. 12)

COOP — Continuity of Operations Plan (Government continuity; Ch. 13)

CONOPS — Concept of Operations (Narrative of how a mission will unfold; Ch. 12)

CONUS — Continental United States (U.S. homeland; Ch. 14)

COP — Combat Outpost (Small forward base; Ch. 12)

CPT — Captain (Company-grade officer; Ch. 3)

CSM — Command Sergeant Major (Senior enlisted advisor; Ch. 9)

C-RAM — Counter-Rocket, Artillery, Mortar (Base-defense system; Ch. 12)

DHS — Department of Homeland Security (Domestic security agency; Ch. 11, 13)

DIA — Defense Intelligence Agency (Military intelligence agency; Ch. 11)

DOD — Department of Defense (U.S. military department; all chapters, anchor Ch. 9)

DODD — Department of Defense Directive (Formal policy; Ch. 13)

DOS — Department of State (U.S. diplomacy arm; Ch. 6, 12)

DOTMLPF-P — Doctrine, Organization, Training, Materiel, Leadership, Personnel, Facilities, Policy (Capability framework; Ch. 16)

DPICM — Dual-Purpose Improved Conventional Munition (Cluster artillery round; Ch. 4–5)

DSM — Diagnostic and Statistical Manual (Clinical guide for mental disorders; Ch. 15)

ECP — Entry Control Point (Access control to bases; Ch. 12)

EOF — Escalation of Force (Stepwise response before lethal force; Ch. 13)

EOD — Explosive Ordnance Disposal (Bomb disposal specialists; Ch. 12)

EW — Electronic Warfare (Use of EM spectrum in conflict; Ch. 16)

FBI — Federal Bureau of Investigation (Domestic investigative agency; Ch. 13)

FEMA — Federal Emergency Management Agency (Disaster response; Ch. 13)

FM — Field Manual (Army doctrinal manual; Ch. 9)

FOB — Forward Operating Base (Larger forward base; Ch. 12)

FRAGO — Fragmentary Order (Update to an existing operations order; Ch. 12)

GAO — Government Accountability Office (Federal watchdog agency; Ch. 10)

GC-HRM — Graduate Certificate in Human Resource Management (Author credential; About the Author)

GEN — General (Four-star officer rank; Ch. 7)

GI Bill — Servicemen's Readjustment Act of 1944 (Veteran education/benefits; Ch. 4)

GOG — Goettge Patrol (Marine recon patrol on Guadalcanal; Ch. 3)

GPS — Global Positioning System (Satellite navigation; Ch. 10, 16)

GWOT — Global War on Terror (Post-9/11 campaign frame; Ch. 11, 12, 14)

HESCO — Hesco Barrier (Wire-and-fill blast wall; Ch. 12)

HMMWV — High Mobility Multipurpose Wheeled Vehicle (Standard GWOT truck; Ch. 12)

HUMINT — Human Intelligence (Person-based intelligence collection; Ch. 16)

HQ — Headquarters (Command node for a formation; Ch. 12)

HR — Human Resources (Personnel management function; Ch. 9)

IA — Individual Augmentee (Augmented Soldier/Airman filling a slot; Ch. 12)

IC — Intelligence Community (Umbrella for CIA, NSA, DIA, etc.; Ch. 11–13)

ICBM — Intercontinental Ballistic Missile (Strategic nuclear missile; Ch. 5)

ICC — International Criminal Court (War-crimes tribunal; Ch. 5)

ICJ — International Court of Justice (UN court for disputes between states; Ch. 13)

ICRC — International Committee of the Red Cross (Neutral aid agency; Ch. 4)

IDF — Indirect Fire (Mortars, rockets, artillery fired from range; Ch. 12)

IED — Improvised Explosive Device (Homemade bomb; Ch. 12)

IJA — Imperial Japanese Army (Japanese ground forces in WWII; Ch. 3, 5)

INTEL — Intelligence (Information for decisions; Ch. 11–12)

IOC — Initial Operating Capability (System/unit minimally ready; Ch. 16)

IO — Information Operations (Coordinated information effects; Ch. 13)

IPB — Intelligence Preparation of the Battlefield (Pre-mission intel analysis; Ch. 12)

IRR — Individual Ready Reserve (Reservists subject to recall; Ch. 12)

ISR — Intelligence, Surveillance, Reconnaissance (Sensor-driven awareness; Ch. 12, 16)

ISAF — International Security Assistance Force (NATO mission in Afghanistan; Ch. 12)

JAG — Judge Advocate General (Military legal corps; Ch. 13)

JCS — Joint Chiefs of Staff (Senior service chiefs panel; Ch. 9)

JDAM — Joint Direct Attack Munition (GPS-guided bomb; Ch. 10, 16)

JP — Joint Publication (Joint-service doctrine; Ch. 9–12)

JSOC — Joint Special Operations Command (Tier-1 SOF headquarters; Ch. 12)

JTAC — Joint Terminal Attack Controller (Ground element controlling air strikes; Ch. 12)

KIA — Killed in Action (Combat fatality; Ch. 3–6)

KSA — Kingdom of Saudi Arabia (Key Gulf state, pre-9/11 context; Ch. 11)

LOAC — Law of Armed Conflict (Legal framework for war conduct; Ch. 5, 13)

LZ — Landing Zone (Designated helicopter landing area; Ch. 8, 12)

MAD — Mutually Assured Destruction (Cold War nuclear deterrent logic; Ch. 5)

MEDEVAC — Medical Evacuation (Movement of wounded; Ch. 3, 12)

METT-TC — Mission, Enemy, Terrain, Troops, Time, Civilians (Planning tool; Ch. 12–13)

MIA — Missing in Action (Unaccounted-for combatant; Ch. 3–5)

MILDEC — Military Deception (Misleading adversary deliberately; Ch. 5, 10)

MILCON — Military Construction (Infrastructure projects for bases; Ch. 12)

MOS — Military Occupational Specialty (Job code; Ch. 9)

MOUT — Military Operations in Urban Terrain (Urban warfare doctrine; Ch. 11)

MRE — Meal, Ready-to-Eat (Field ration; Ch. 12)

MRAP — Mine-Resistant Ambush Protected Vehicle (IED-resistant truck; Ch. 12)

MSR — Main Supply Route (Key logistical road; Ch. 12)

MST — Military Sexual Trauma (Service-related sexual violence; Ch. 15)

NARA — National Archives and Records Administration (Records repository; Ch. 1–7)

NATO — North Atlantic Treaty Organization (Western alliance; Ch. 5, 12)

NBC — National Broadcasting Company (Major U.S. broadcaster; Ch. 1)

NCO — Non-Commissioned Officer (Enlisted leader; Ch. 9)

NGO — Non-Governmental Organization (Humanitarian/development groups; Ch. 7, 12)

NIH — National Institutes of Health (Medical research, trauma context; Ch. 15)

NIIT — Net Investment Income Tax (Financial term in economic analysis; Appendix)

NSA — National Security Agency (Signals intelligence agency; Ch. 11–12)

OEF — Operation Enduring Freedom (War in Afghanistan; Ch. 12)

OIF — Operation Iraqi Freedom (War in Iraq; Ch. 12)

OODA Loop — Observe, Orient, Decide, Act (Decision cycle; Ch. 10, 16)

OP — Observation Post (Small surveillance position; Ch. 12)

OPLAN — Operations Plan (Formal plan for major ops; Ch. 12)

OPORD — Operations Order (Directive to execute a mission; Ch. 12)

OPSEC — Operations Security (Protecting critical info; Ch. 13)

OSINT — Open-Source Intelligence (Public-source intel; Ch. 13, 16)

PAO — Public Affairs Office (Media interface for units/DoD; Ch. 1, 13)

PAX — Personnel (Headcount shorthand; Ch. 12)

PCC — Pre-Combat Check (Initial readiness check; Ch. 12)

PCI — Pre-Combat Inspection (Leader-level detailed check; Ch. 12)

PFC — Private First Class (Junior enlisted rank; Ch. 3, 12)

PKI — Public Key Infrastructure (Encryption/authentication framework; Ch. 16)

POG — Person Other than Grunt (Slang for non-infantry troops; Ch. 2, 12)

POW — Prisoner of War (Captured combatant; Ch. 3, 6)

PPE — Personal Protective Equipment (Protective gear; Ch. 12)

PSYOP — Psychological Operations (Influence and perception ops; Ch. 13)

PT Belt — Physical Training Reflective Belt (Safety belt, symbol of bureaucracy; Ch. 9)

PTSD — Post-Traumatic Stress Disorder (War-related trauma diagnosis; Ch. 6, 12, 15)

QRF — Quick Reaction Force (Rapid-response force; Ch. 12)

QM — Quartermaster (Supply/logistics branch; Ch. 12)

RFI — Request for Information (Formal question for clarification; Ch. 12)

ROE — Rules of Engagement (Legal limits on force; Ch. 12, 13)

RPG — Rocket-Propelled Grenade (Shoulder-fired explosive; Ch. 12)

RTO — Radio Telephone Operator (Radio operator on patrol; Ch. 12)

S-1 — Personnel Staff Section (Admin & personnel; Ch. 9)

S-2 — Intelligence Staff Section (Threat/intel; Ch. 12)

S-3 — Operations Staff Section (Plans & current ops; Ch. 12)

S-3/5 — Operations & Plans (Combined) (Fused ops/future plans; Ch. 12)

S-3/7 — Operations & Training (Combined) (Ops with training management; Ch. 12)

S-3/9 — Operations & Civil Affairs / Engineer Effects (CA in maneuver, effects in engineers; Ch. 12, author background)

S-4 — Logistics Staff Section (Supply & sustainment; Ch. 12)

S-5 — Plans Staff Section (Future ops planning; Ch. 12)

S-6 — Signal Staff Section (Comms & networks; Ch. 12, 16)

S-7 — Information Operations / Training (IO or training cell; Ch. 13)

S-8 — Finance / Resource Management (Budget & resourcing; Ch. 12)

S-9 — Civil Affairs OR Engineer Effects (CA/maneuver or EN effects; Ch. 12, author role)

SIGACT — Significant Activity Report (Recorded incident/event; Ch. 12)

SIGINT — Signals Intelligence (Intercepted communications; Ch. 11–12)

SITREP — Situation Report (Short status summary; Ch. 12)

SME — Subject Matter Expert (Specialized knowledge holder; Ch. 9)

SOP — Standard Operating Procedure (Established method; Ch. 12)

SS — Schutzstaffel (Nazi paramilitary apparatus; Ch. 5)

STB — Special Troops Battalion (Mixed-support battalion; Ch. 12)

TACSOP — Tactical Standard Operating Procedure (Unit tactical SOP; Ch. 12)

TBI — Traumatic Brain Injury (Brain injury from blast/impact; Ch. 12, 15)

TIC — Troops in Contact (Radio call indicating active firefight; Ch. 12)

TLP — Troop Leading Procedures (Small-unit planning steps; Ch. 12)

TOC — Tactical Operations Center (Unit battle command hub; Ch. 12)

TPU — Troop Program Unit (Army Reserve) (Reserve unit structure; Ch. 12)

TTP — Tactics, Techniques, and Procedures (Practical "how-to" for combat; Ch. 11, 12)

UAS — Unmanned Aircraft System (Full drone system; Ch. 16)

UAV — Unmanned Aerial Vehicle (Drone aircraft; Ch. 16)

UC — Unified Command (Integrated multi-agency command; Ch. 13)

UCMJ — Uniform Code of Military Justice (Military legal code; Ch. 13)

UK — United Kingdom (WWII ally & NATO partner; Ch. 4, 12)

UN — United Nations (Post-WWII international body; Ch. 4, 6)

UNESCO — UN Educational, Scientific and Cultural Organization (Protects heritage & culture; Ch. 5)

UNHCR — UN High Commissioner for Refugees (Refugee support agency; Ch. 7, 12)

USA — United States Army (Land force; Ch. 3–12)

USAF — United States Air Force (Air arm of U.S. military; Ch. 10, 13)

USAR — United States Army Reserve (Reserve land component; Ch. 12)

USMC — United States Marine Corps (Expeditionary force; Ch. 3, 12)

USN — United States Navy (Maritime force; Ch. 3, 10)

VA — Department of Veterans Affairs (Veteran healthcare & benefits; Ch. 14–15)

VFW — Veterans of Foreign Wars (Veterans' organization & social hub; Ch. 14)

VWCWG — Vietnam War Crimes Working Group (Pentagon war-crimes archive; Ch. 6)

WWI — World War I (1914–1918 global war; Ch. 3, 5)

WWII — World War II (1939–1945 global war; Ch. 1–5)

NASA — National Aeronautics and Space Administration (Civil space/tech agency; Ch. 16)

NFL — National Football League (Professional football league; Ch. 2 "Salute to Service")

NYPD — New York Police Department (Referenced in domestic security/terror context; Ch. 11–13 themed)

DHS-FEMA — DHS/FEMA Combined Context (Homeland security & disaster response structure; Ch. 11, 13)

ISR Stack — Layered ISR Coverage (Multiple ISR platforms over target area; Ch. 16)

Glossary of Key Terms and Concepts

This glossary is offered for readers who may not speak the languages of uniform, policy, or trauma. Many of these terms have evolved across generations, carrying both official meaning and personal weight. Where doctrine defines procedure, experience defines consequence. These brief explanations aim to clarify not only what the words mean—but what they cost.

1. All-Volunteer Force (AVF) — The post-1973 U.S. military model that eliminated the draft and replaced it with career service, concentrating the burden of war onto a small warrior caste. It created unmatched professionalism but widened the civil–military divide.

First appears Ch. 9; also Ch. 12; conceptually Ch. 14.

2. Amnesia of War — The recurring national pattern of forgetting painful lessons once the parades end, allowing future wars to be justified by optimism rather than memory. This erasure ensures that each generation inherits the consequences of lessons never learned.

First appears Ch. 1; conceptually Ch. 16.

3. Ashli Babbitt Funeral Controversy — The event in which military honors were granted to a veteran killed while breaching the Capitol on Jan. 6, reopening the debate on what constitutes honorable service. This controversy exposed fractures in national identity and trust in institutions.

First appears Ch. 13.

4. Battle of Xuân Lộc — South Vietnam's final major stand in April 1975, a desperate defense that momentarily held back collapse. It symbolized heroic resistance against inevitability.

First appears Ch. 7.

5. Civil–Military Gap — The widening separation between American society and its armed forces, driven by the end of the draft and generational isolation from service. This gap fuels misunderstanding, polarization, and moral distance.

First appears Ch. 2; also Ch. 9; conceptually Ch. 12–14.

6. Civil Religion — The merging of patriotic symbols with sacred meaning, creating rituals that elevate military sacrifice into national theology. It comforts the grieving but can shield hard truths behind ceremony.

First appears Ch. 1.

7. Collateral Damage — The sanitized phrase used to describe civilian deaths caused by military action. Its euphemistic nature conceals the true human cost behind technical language.

First appears Ch. 4; conceptually Ch. 10 & 12.

8. Command Responsibility — The doctrine holding leaders accountable for the actions or failures of their subordinates. It is the moral spine that prevents war from sliding fully into chaos.

First appears Ch. 5; strongly in Ch. 13.

9. Containment — The Cold War strategy that used limited war and alliances to prevent communist expansion. Its rigid framework trapped the U.S. in Vietnam's unwinnable logic.

First appears Ch. 6.

10. Dehumanization — The psychological act of reducing the enemy to an object, enabling killing while delaying emotional consequence. It protects in combat but wounds in memory.

First appears Ch. 3; appears conceptually in Ch. 6 & Ch. 12.

11. Draft Lottery — The Vietnam-era conscription method that turned birthdays into destiny. It became a symbol of inequality and moral fracture.

First appears Ch. 6.

12. Electronic Barrier (McNamara's Line) — A Vietnam-era electronic sensor grid meant to automate detection of enemy movement, foreshadowing today's AI warfare. It promised clarity but delivered confusion.

First appears Ch. 6; later referenced Ch. 16.

13. Free-Fire Zone — An area where any movement could be legally engaged, collapsing moral distinctions between civilian and combatant. It epitomized Vietnam's drift into systemic atrocity.

First appears Ch. 6.

14. Generational Inheritance — The transfer of trauma, silence, or coping habits from veterans to their families. Children often carry the emotional aftermath of battles they never saw.

First appears Ch. 1; deeply in Ch. 14.

15. Global War on Terror (GWOT) — The vast post-9/11 campaign fought by a small volunteer force on behalf of an entire nation. It became both the longest war in American history and the least shared.

First appears Ch. 12; conceptually tied Ch. 14.

16. Goettge Patrol — A Marine reconnaissance patrol annihilated on Guadalcanal, illustrating the lethal miscalculations of early Pacific warfare. Its destruction became a symbol of American unpreparedness.

First appears Ch. 3.

17. Hollywood – Pentagon Partnership — The decades-long collaboration where Hollywood receives equipment and access, and the Pentagon shapes war narratives. It blurs the line between memory and marketing.

First appears Ch. 1; also Ch. 8.

18. Moral Discipline — The internal boundary that prevents obedience from becoming blind obedience. It keeps lethal authority tied to conscience.

First appears Ch. 3; central again in Ch. 13.

19. Moral Injury — The invisible wound caused not by fear, but by actions or betrayals that violated one's moral core. Unlike PTSD, it is a spiritual dislocation rather than purely psychological trauma.

First appears Ch. 6; appears Ch. 12 & 15.

20. Moral Resilience — The process of reclaiming moral clarity after war breaks it. It requires honesty, accountability, and connection rather than denial.

First appears Ch. 12; tied Ch. 14.

21. Moral Silence — The survival instinct to protect loved ones from the truth by withholding it. Over time, that silence becomes its own burden.

First appears Ch. 1; deeply in Ch. 14.

22. National Will — The collective endurance required to sustain war. It is strong under clarity and dissolves under confusion or political fracture.

First appears Ch. 9; appears Ch. 12; conceptually Ch. 16.

23. Operational Fatigue — The spiritual and mental exhaustion produced not just by combat, but by relentless uncertainty, deployment cycles, and vigilance. It erodes judgment long before it breaks the body.

First appears Ch. 12; in Ch. 14.

24. Propaganda — The shaping of perception through symbols, images, and messaging that simplifies conflict into morality play. It molds public memory long after the facts fade.

First appears Ch. 1; strong in Ch. 5 & Ch. 13.

25. PTSD (Post-Traumatic Stress Disorder) — A psychological condition marked by intrusive memories, hypervigilance, nightmares, and emotional numbness. It is the brain's attempt to survive an event that the soul has not yet understood or accepted.

First appears Ch. 6; also in Ch. 12 & Ch. 14.

26. Rules of Engagement (ROE) — The legal and moral framework that defines when force may be used. It prevents combat from collapsing into chaos and protects Soldiers from both hesitation and excess.

First appears Ch. 13.

27. Silence of Return — The inability for veterans to translate battle into civilian language, resulting in isolation rather than reintegration. Silence becomes both shield and prison.

First appears Ch. 14.

28. Strategic Illusion — The belief that technology or precision can eliminate the moral fog of war. It seduces leaders into thinking war can be clean when experience proves otherwise.

First appears Ch. 10; tied to Ch. 16.

29. Technological Amnesia — The dangerous confidence that machines will solve ethical dilemmas humans have never mastered. It erases past warnings under the promise of innovation.

First appears Ch. 16.

30. The Pipeline — The cultural channel of sports, schools, and family tradition that funnels young Americans into military service. It replaces the draft with subtle expectation.

First appears Ch. 2; also Ch. 9 & Ch. 12.

31. Total War — A conflict in which whole societies, not just armies, are mobilized and targeted. It blurs the line between civilian and combatant, leaving entire populations devastated.

First appears Ch. 1; again Ch. 4 & Ch. 5.

32. Winter Soldier — A term revived in 1971 when Vietnam veterans testified about war crimes and moral injury. It symbolizes the courage to confront the nation with truths it prefers to ignore.

First appears Ch. 6.

33. Guadalcanal Campaign — The brutal WWII island offensive that forced America to relearn the ferocity of modern war. Hunger, disease, and night assaults defined the campaign as much as bullets.

First appears Ch. 3.

34. The Language of Targets — The linguistic shift that turns human beings into objects — silhouettes, hostiles, collateral — to make killing psychologically manageable. It numbs conscience while sharpening reflexes.

First appears Ch. 3.

35. Banzai Charges — Desperate mass assaults by Japanese forces, marked by suicidal bravery and absolute resolve. These attacks shattered illusions about quick victory in the Pacific.

First appears Ch. 3.

36. Henderson Field — The strategic airfield on Guadalcanal whose defense became a defining struggle of the early Pacific war. Whoever controlled the runway controlled the island's fate.

First appears Ch. 3.

37. Okinawa Campaign — One of WWII's bloodiest battles, marked by civilian tragedy, cave warfare, and relentless artillery. It revealed the terrifying cost of fighting an enemy unwilling to surrender.

First appears Ch. 3; conceptually throughout Part I.

38. Bocage (Normandy Hedgerows) — Dense earthen barriers that turned Normandy into a maze of kill zones. Troops fought at point-blank range, making liberation slow and brutal.

First appears Ch. 4.

39. Falaise Pocket — The encirclement of German forces in Normandy that ended with horrific destruction. Corpses, animals, and wreckage littered the battlefield for miles, a reminder of victory's cost.

First appears Ch. 4.

40. Caen Bombardment — The Allied destruction of Caen in the name of liberation, flattening a historic city and killing thousands of civilians. It exposed the paradox of "saving" a place by destroying it.

First appears Ch. 4.

41. Saint-Lô Destruction — The near-erasure of a French town during Normandy operations, known later as "the capital of ruins." Liberation came wrapped in fire.

First appears Ch. 4.

42. Tarawa Assault — A three-day Pacific battle that cost over a thousand Marine lives and foreshadowed the horrors of amphibious assaults yet to come. Survivors carried its scars for decades.

First appears Ch. 15.

43. Amphibious Warfare (WWII) — The lethal combination of sea, sand, and enemy fire that defined Pacific operations. These landings produced some of the war's highest casualties in the shortest time.

First appears Ch. 3 & Ch. 4.

44. Firebombing Doctrine — The WWII policy of burning cities to break enemy industry and will, used in Tokyo, Dresden, and Hamburg. It revealed the dark symmetry between Allied necessity and destruction.

First appears Ch. 4 & Ch. 5.

45. Nanking Massacre — The six-week atrocity where Japanese forces slaughtered hundreds of thousands of civilians. Its horror was amplified by the world's indifference.

First appears Ch. 5.

46. Einsatzgruppen — Mobile Nazi killing units that executed over a million civilians before the gas chambers existed. They proved that genocide does not begin with technology, but with obedience.

First appears Ch. 5.

47. The Holocaust (as System) — The industrialized, bureaucratic annihilation of entire peoples, carried out with chilling efficiency. It was mass murder transformed into administrative routine.

First appears Ch. 5.

48. Re-education Camps (Vietnam) — Postwar prisons where South Vietnamese officers and officials were tortured, starved, and "retrained." They were instruments of political erasure as much as punishment.

First appears Ch. 7.

49. Dien Bien Phu — The decisive 1954 battle where French forces were encircled and annihilated by Vietnamese revolutionaries, ending French colonial rule in Indochina. It exposed the futility of trying to impose empire on people fighting for their own history.

First appears Ch. 6.

50. Geneva Accords (1954) — The international agreement that divided Vietnam at the 17th parallel and promised elections that never came. Its failure guaranteed the next twenty years of conflict.

First appears Ch. 6.

51. Domino Theory — The Cold War belief that if one nation fell to communism, the rest would follow. This simplified logic dragged the U.S. deeper into wars it did not understand.

First appears Ch. 6.

52. Strategic Hamlets Program — The South Vietnamese and U.S. policy of relocating entire villages behind fortified perimeters to isolate the Viet Cong. Instead of winning hearts and minds, it uprooted them.

Conceptually referenced Ch. 6.

53. Search-and-Destroy Operations — U.S. missions designed to find enemy forces, kill them, and withdraw without holding ground. They turned the war into a cycle of attrition without strategy.

First appears Ch. 6; also in Winter Soldier discussion.

54. Body Count Metrics — The Vietnam-era practice of measuring success by enemy deaths rather than strategic gain. It rewarded killing over understanding and drove systemic brutality.

First appears Ch. 6.

55. Free Fire Doctrine (Vietnam) — A permissive engagement policy that allowed U.S. forces to strike without verifying targets. It blurred the line between combat and atrocity.

First appears Ch. 6 (variant of Free-Fire Zone).

56. Rolling Thunder — The sustained U.S. bombing campaign against North Vietnam intended to break enemy will. Instead, it hardened it and devastated civilians.

Conceptually referenced Ch. 6.

57. Project 100,000 — The Vietnam-era program that drafted men with lower aptitude scores to fill manpower needs, sending many unprepared into combat. It exposed the dark arithmetic of wartime bureaucracy.

First appears Ch. 6; expanded in Ch. 8.

58. Operation Ranch Hand (Defoliation) — The aerial spraying of herbicides like Agent Orange meant to expose enemy positions. It sowed environmental destruction and generational illness.

Referenced conceptually Ch. 6.

59. The Draft & The Exodus — The wave of draft resistance that sent tens of thousands of Americans to Canada, Sweden, and elsewhere. It revealed a nation divided not only by policy but by conscience.

First appears Ch. 6.

60. Vietnamization — The Nixon-era policy of shifting combat responsibility to South Vietnamese forces while withdrawing U.S. troops. In practice, it was a slow handoff of collapse.

Conceptually referenced Ch. 6 & Ch. 7.

61. Fall of Saigon (1975) — The chaotic end of the Vietnam War marked by helicopter evacuations, desperate crowds, and the collapse of a nation left alone. It became the symbol of American strategic failure.

First appears Ch. 7.

62. Mogadishu, 1993 — The urban firefight known as "Black Hawk Down," where U.S. forces faced overwhelming militia resistance. Its televised aftermath shaped American caution for a decade.

First appears Ch. 11.

63. U.S. Embassy Bombings (1998) — Al-Qaeda's near-simultaneous attacks on U.S. embassies in Kenya and Tanzania, killing hundreds. It was a clear warning of a global terror threat the world ignored.

First appears Ch. 11.

64. USS Cole Bombing (2000) — The suicide attack on a U.S. Navy destroyer refueling in Yemen, killing 17 sailors. It marked a direct strike on American force projection in the Middle East.

First appears Ch. 11.

65. September 11 Attacks — Coordinated hijackings that killed nearly 3,000 people and plunged the U.S. into the longest war in its history. It shattered illusions of safety and remade global strategy overnight.

First appears Ch. 12.

66. Operation Enduring Freedom (OEF) — The initial U.S. invasion of Afghanistan to dismantle al-Qaeda and remove the Taliban. What began in clarity evolved into a generational conflict without victory.

First appears Ch. 12.

67. Operation Iraqi Freedom (OIF) — The 2003 U.S. invasion of Iraq launched under flawed intelligence and expansive ambition. It became one of America's most politically divisive wars.

First appears Ch. 12.

68. Khōgyani District (Afghanistan) — A rural valley where Taliban fighters used terrain, patience, and fear to undermine U.S. outposts. It embodied the endurance and brutality of insurgent warfare.

First appears Ch. 12.

69. Forward Operating Base / Outpost Dynamics — The isolated strongpoints that became both lifelines and targets for U.S. forces. These posts magnified fear, vigilance, and the psychological grind of modern war.

First appears Ch. 12.

70. Indirect Fire (Mortars/Rockets) — The unseen threat of incoming rounds that defined daily life in Afghanistan and Iraq. The silence before impact became its own kind of terror.

First appears Ch. 12.

71. Drone Warfare (Predator/Sensor Age) — The use of unmanned aircraft to surveil and strike enemies with precision. It distanced kill from conscience and ushered in a new moral frontier.

First appears Ch. 16; conceptually tied to Ch. 12.

72. Lone Survivor Incident / Operation Red Wings — The compromised SEAL mission in Kunar where a decision to release civilians led to catastrophe. It illustrates the impossible moral dilemmas of counterinsurgency.

First appears Ch. 12.

73. North Korea Fishing Vessel Incident — A covert maritime mission where U.S. special operations forces killed civilian witnesses to avoid geopolitical escalation. It remains a stark example of how clandestine warfare pushes operators into ethical dead zones.

First appears Ch. 12.

74. January 6 Capitol Breach — The violent assault on the U.S. Capitol in an attempt to overturn an election, revealing deep fractures in American democratic resilience. It exposed failures in command, intelligence, and preparedness.

First appears Ch. 13.

75. Failure of Command (January 6 ROE Breakdown) — The systemic collapse of leadership that left front-line officers without clarity, equipment, or authority to respond. It demonstrated how hesitation at the top becomes chaos at the bottom.

First appears Ch. 13.

76. Domestic ROE / Riot Control Protocols — The legal framework governing force inside U.S. borders. When unclear, it paralyzes defenders and allows mobs to dictate the terms of conflict.

First appears Ch. 13.

77. Moral Paralysis — The opposite of desensitization — a state where excessive restraint prevents necessary action. It appears when fear of wrongdoing outweighs survival instinct.

Conceptually present Ch. 12 & Ch. 13.

78. Vietnam Syndrome — The national reluctance to engage in prolonged foreign wars after Vietnam, driven by public distrust in leaders and strategy. It shaped policy for decades until shattered by 9/11.

First appears Ch. 6; referenced throughout Part II & III.

79. Post-Vietnam Syndrome — An early conceptual forerunner to PTSD, described by clinicians as the lingering moral, emotional, and psychological injuries carried by Vietnam veterans. It captured wounds before language existed to name them.

First appears Ch. 6.

80. Secondary Trauma (Family Trauma) — The emotional and behavioral effects experienced by families of veterans. Children inherit the silence, anger, or emptiness brought home from war.

First appears Ch. 14.

81. Intergenerational Silence — The quiet transmission of unspoken war memories across generations. Trauma echoes most loudly in what parents never say.

First appears Ch. 14.

82. Suicide as a Continuation of War — The idea that many veterans do not die in the war, but because of it — months, years, or decades later. Suicide becomes the final casualty of battles long past.

First appears Ch. 15.

83. Memory as Doctrine — The phenomenon where public memory of war becomes the blueprint for future wars — often sanitized, simplified, or weaponized. It shapes national identity more than facts.

Conceptually referenced Ch. 1, Ch. 8, Ch. 16.

84. Precision-Guided Munitions (PGM Revolution) — Weapons that dramatically increased accuracy during conflicts like Desert Storm, encouraging the belief that war could be clean. Precision did not remove suffering — it hid it behind spectacle.

First appears Ch. 10.

85. Revolution in Military Affairs (RMA) — The belief that technology fundamentally transforms the nature of war. In practice, it often inflates confidence faster than it improves judgment.

First appears Ch. 10; tied Ch. 16.

86. AI-Assisted Targeting — The use of algorithms to identify, track, or recommend lethal targets in real time. It accelerates decisions beyond human emotional or ethical thresholds.

First appears Ch. 16.

87. Cyber/Information Battlespace — The domain where propaganda, hacking, and information warfare shape perception before bullets ever fly. Modern conflict begins online long before it erupts on land.

Conceptual in Ch. 13 & Ch. 16.

88. Drone-Enabled Surveillance — The persistent monitoring of battlefields by unmanned systems that see everything but understand nothing. It creates omnipresence without empathy.

First appears Ch. 16.

89. Sensors-as-Weaponry — The concept that detection itself becomes lethal when connected to automated strike systems. It began with McNamara's Line and matured into today's autonomous platforms.

First appears Ch. 16.

90. Sports-Military Pipeline — The cultural pipeline linking athletic discipline to military service. It conditions youth to accept hierarchy, toughness, and sacrifice long before enlistment.

First appears Ch. 2; expanded Ch. 9.

91. Media Spectacle Warfare (CNN Effect) — The phenomenon where televised war shapes perception more than battlefield reality. It influences policy by making conflict seem cleaner or more chaotic than it is.

First appears Ch. 10; referenced Ch. 11.

92. Desert Storm Illusion — The belief, born in 1991, that war could be fast, bloodless, and decisive. This illusion set the stage for the long, grinding wars that followed.

First appears Ch. 10; conceptually tied Ch. 12.

93. **Shadow Wars** (1990s Terror Era) — The decade-long pattern of attacks, bombings, and covert battles leading up to 9/11. These warnings were ignored by a nation convinced it was untouchable.

First appears Ch. 11.

94. **The Echo of Elah** — The phenomenon where war's consequences follow Soldiers home long after deployment, eroding families and identities. It is the quiet war within the walls of the home.

First appears Ch. 12.

95. **Suicide Bombing / Asymmetric Tactics** — The strategy of using small, committed cells to inflict massive psychological and strategic impact. It exploits moral restraint and magnifies fear.

First appears Ch. 11; tied Ch. 12.

96. **Insurgency vs. Counterinsurgency (COIN)** — The clash between forces that hide within populations and armies trying to defeat them without destroying civilians. It is war fought in the moral gray zone.

First appears Ch. 12; throughout Ch. 6 & 13 conceptually.

Top Names Mentioned in This Book or Referenced:

1. **Aidid, Mohamed Farrah**

   Aidid turned Mogadishu into the graveyard of American assumptions in 1993, proving that a militia with patience and home-ground cunning could bleed a superpower. His fighters taught the U.S. that war is fought as much in alleys and stairwells as on open fields.

   War/Period: Somalia, 1993. **Appears:** Ch. 11. **Also:** Asymmetric warfare precursor.

2. **Anderson, Lars**

   Anderson's history of the Thorpe-Eisenhower football clash reveals how American toughness was shaped in stadiums long before it was tested on battlefields. His work underlines NTOT's connection between athletic culture and military ethos.

   War/Period: Pre-WWI/WWII cultural era. **Appears:** Ch. 2. **Also:** Sports–service pipeline.

3. **Ashli Babbitt**

   A GWOT-era Air Force veteran whose death during the Capitol breach became a lightning rod for rival narratives of patriotism and betrayal. Her military funeral honors forced the nation to confront the meaning of service in a fractured Republic.

War/Period: GWOT-era USAF. **Appears:** Ch. 13. **Also:** Civil–military identity fracture.

4. **Joe Biden**

   A Cold War politician invoking WWII heroism at Pointe du Hoc in 2024, Biden's rhetoric shows how modern leaders reinterpret old sacrifices to address new dilemmas.
   War/Period: Cold War → GWOT era. **Appears:** Ch. 4. **Also:** Political memory usage.

5. **James G. Blight**

   A historian who helped McNamara confront the moral failures of Vietnam decades too late. Blight's work exposes the tragic distance between policy intention and consequence.
   War/Period: Vietnam reassessment. **Appears:** Ch. 6. **Also:** Technocratic illusions.

6. **Mark Bowden**

   Bowden's *Black Hawk Down* captured the terror and chaos of Mogadishu, stripping away illusions of clean modern warfare. His work became the definitive civilian portrait of 1990s urban combat.
   War/Period: Somalia, 1993. **Appears:** Ch. 11. **Also:** Modern urban battle lessons.

7. **George H.W. Bush**

   A WWII aviator who survived being shot down and later commanded Desert Storm, Bush bridged two eras—bloody attrition and clean, televised precision.

   War/Period: WWII & Gulf War. **Appears:** Ch. 10. **Also:** Desert Storm illusion.

8. **George W. Bush**

   President on 9/11 whose decisions launched Afghanistan and Iraq, shaping a generation's war. His leadership forms the backbone of the GWOT era examined in NTOT.

   War/Period: Afghanistan/Iraq. **Appears:** Ch. 12. **Also:** National will patterns.

9. **Frank Capra**

   Director of *Why We Fight*, Capra helped create America's righteous-war narrative, cementing WWII as moral mythology.

   War/Period: WWII. **Appears:** Ch. 1. **Also:** Hollywood–Pentagon roots.

10. **Philip Caputo**

    Marine lieutenant whose memoir *A Rumor of War* was among the first raw testimonies of Vietnam's moral unraveling. His voice captures the disillusionment beneath official rhetoric.

    War/Period: Vietnam. **Appears:** Ch. 15. **Also:** Moral injury testimony.

11. **Jimmy Carter**

Post-Vietnam president who sought moral leadership in a nation exhausted by conflict. His era marks a transition between disillusionment and recovery.

War/Period: Post-Vietnam Cold War. **Appears:** Contextually Part II. **Also:** National healing.

12. **Bill Clinton**

President during Mogadishu, embassy bombings, and USS Cole —the shadow decade leading to 9/11. His responses illus-trate America's failure to recognize rising threats.

War/Period: 1990s Shadow War. **Appears:** Ch. 11. **Also:** Terror prelude.

13. **Francis Ford Coppola**

His *Apocalypse Now* portrayed Vietnam as psychological descent rather than geographic conflict. Coppola's surrealism became cultural testimony to moral collapse.

War/Period: Vietnam memory. **Appears:** Ch. 8. **Also:** Myth vs. madness.

14. **Walter Donahue**

WWII radiology technician and later Vi-etnam AMA physician —who healed across two wars. His story embodies compassion under fire and generational inheritance.

War/Period: WWII & Vietnam. **Appears:** Ch. 1, 4. **Also:** Medical burden of war.

15. **Anton Drexler**

Founder of the political club that became the Nazi Party, Drexler shows how fringe resentment can become catastrophic history.

War/Period: Pre-WWII. **Appears:** Ch. 5. **Also:** Extremism origins.

16. **Dietrich Eckart**

Poet and nationalist who shaped Hitler's rhetoric, proving that cultural figures often architect atrocities long before Soldiers carry them out.

War/Period: Pre-WWII. **Appears:** Ch. 5. **Also:** Ideological radicalization.

17. **Dwight D. Eisenhower**

From Army halfback to Supreme Allied Commander, Eisenhower embodied disciplined leadership across war and peace. His dual legacy shows the fusion of athletic and military culture.

War/Period: WWII & Cold War. **Appears:** Ch. 2, 4. **Also:** Sports pipeline.

18. **Elie Wiesel**

    A survivor who transformed atrocity into moral memory, Wiesel forces readers to confront the human meaning behind the statistics of genocide.

    War/Period: WWII/Holocaust. **Appears:** Ch. 5. **Also:** Conscience of memory.

19. **Frances Fitzgerald**

    Her book *Fire in the Lake* exposed America's profound misreading of Vietnam, showing that cultural ignorance can kill as effectively as weapons.

    War/Period: Vietnam analysis. **Appears:** Part II. **Also:** Strategic misunderstandings.

20. **John Ford**

    WWII filmmaker whose combat footage shaped national memory of the "Good War." Ford's realism anchored the mythology of courage and sacrifice.

    War/Period: WWII. **Appears:** Ch. 1. **Also:** Propaganda shaping.

21. **Joe Galloway**

    The journalist who fought beside Soldiers in Ia Drang; his writing brought Vietnam's earliest truths home with painful clarity.

    War/Period: Vietnam. **Appears:** Ch. 8. **Also:** Ground truth witness.

22. **Mark Harris**

    Historian of *Five Came Back*, chronicling the directors who captured WWII's soul on film. His work reveals how memory is curated.

    War/Period: WWII cultural memory. **Appears:** Ch. 1. **Also:** Narrative shaping.

23. **Wade J. Hart**

    Okinawa veteran whose silence carried the war into the next generations. His life anchors NTOT's central argument about inherited burden.

    War/Period: WWII (Pacific). **Appears:** Ch. 1, 3, 14. **Also:** Family inheritance.

24. **Chris Hedges**

    A war correspondent whose writing exposes conflict's seductive and destructive psychology. His insights give NTOT its philosophical backbone.

    War/Period: Multiple conflicts. **Appears:** Ch. 5. **Also:** War's moral gravity.

25. **Paul Haggis**

    Director of *In the Valley of Elah*, whose film captures the quiet, psychological collapse of GWOT veterans confronting themselves after battle.

War/Period: Iraq/Afghanistan (cultural). **Appears:** Ch. 12. **Also:** Silence of return.

26. **Adolf Hitler**

Architect of WWII and the Holocaust, Hitler turned bureaucracy, myth, and obedience into instruments of extermination. His regime remains the benchmark for industrial evil. **War/Period:** WWII. **Appears:** Ch. 5. **Also:** Machinery of murder.

27. **Ho Chi Minh**

The anti-colonial revolutionary who defeated France, resisted Japan, and outlasted the United States. His nationalism was misread as monolithic communism, fueling an unwinnable war. **War/Period:** First Indochina → Vietnam. **Appears:** Ch. 6. **Also:** Strategic misunderstanding.

28. **John Huston**

His suppressed WWII documentary *Let There Be Light* captured the psychological wounds of Soldiers long before PTSD had a name.

War/Period: WWII. **Appears:** Ch. 1. **Also:** Early trauma testimony.

29. **John F. Kennedy**

War hero turned statesman whose early Vietnam decisions set America on a path of slow escalation. Kennedy's optimism and faith in expertise became tragic illusions.

War/Period: WWII (PT-109) → Vietnam. **Appears:** Ch. 6. **Also:** "Best and Brightest" arc.

30. **John Kerry**

Decorated Vietnam veteran who later testified to Congress about war crimes, becoming a lightning rod for truth-telling. His courage challenged both sides of the conflict.

War/Period: Vietnam. **Appears:** Ch. 6. **Also:** Winter Soldier ethos.

31. **Ron Kovic**

A Marine paralyzed in Vietnam who turned his pain into protest, Kovic symbolizes the path from patriotic devotion to moral confrontation.

War/Period: Vietnam. **Appears:** Ch. 8. **Also:** Homefront trauma.

32. **Jon Krakauer**

His investigation into Pat Tillman's death revealed the institutional pressures that distort wartime truth. Krakauer's work exposes the fragility of trust.

War/Period: GWOT. **Appears:** Ch. 12. **Also:** Institutional integrity themes.

33. **Chris Kyle**

The Iraq War's most public sniper—lionized and criticized in equal measure—Kyle represents the modern myth of the precision warrior in America's imagination.

War/Period: Iraq. **Appears:** Ch. 12. **Also:** Heroism vs. narrative.

34. **Robert Jay Lifton**

Psychiatrist whose research on veterans exposed the hidden wounds of war and helped define the language of moral injury.

War/Period: Vietnam-era trauma. **Appears:** Ch. 6. **Also:** Psychological frameworks.

35. **Brett T. Litz**

A leading psychologist who formalized the concept of moral injury, giving scientific grounding to wounds that medicine alone cannot treat.

War/Period: Post-Vietnam → GWOT research. **Appears:** Ch. 12–14. **Also:** Invisible wounds.

36. **Matthew Lohmeier**

Air Force official whose authorization of military honors for

Ashli Babbitt challenged the boundaries of loyalty and the meaning of service.

War/Period: GWOT-era USAF. **Appears:** Ch. 13. **Also:** Civil–military crisis.

37. **Marcus Luttrell**

The lone survivor of Operation Red Wings whose escape illustrated both the brutality and moral ambiguity of counterinsurgency warfare.

War/Period: Afghanistan. **Appears:** Ch. 12. **Also:** ROE dilemmas.

38. **Terrence Malick**

Director of *The Thin Red Line*, whose lyrical interpretation of Guadalcanal transformed brutality into meditation, revealing war's spiritual wounds.

War/Period: WWII (film). **Appears:** Ch. 3, 8. **Also:** War and soul.

39. **Mao Zedong**

His Cultural Revolution and Great Leap Forward killed tens of millions, proving that ideology can become deadlier than any enemy army.

War/Period: Chinese Civil War → Cultural Revolution. **Appears:** Ch. 5. **Also:** State terror.

40. **Karl Mayr**

Army intelligence officer who recognized Hitler's rhetorical power and inadvertently set him on a path to domination. Mayr reminds us institutions can midwife monsters.

War/Period: Post-WWI. **Appears:** Ch. 5. **Also:** Radicalization mechanism.

41. **Robert S. McNamara**

The technocrat who tried to quantize war, reducing Vietnam to numbers while ignoring meaning. His late-life regret embodies the tragedy of analytic hubris.

War/Period: Vietnam. **Appears:** Ch. 6, 16. **Also:** Technological amnesia.

42. **Hal Moore**

Commander at Ia Drang, Moore represents leadership grounded in discipline and humanity amid chaos—the best of what Vietnam demanded but rarely allowed.

War/Period: Vietnam. **Appears:** Ch. 8. **Also:** Leadership under fire.

43. **Sarah Haley**

One of the first clinicians courageous enough to document sexual assault and trauma among Vietnam veterans, Haley gave vocabulary to wounds no one wanted to acknowledge.

War/Period: Vietnam trauma. **Appears:** Ch. 6. **Also:** PTSD conceptual development.

44. **Osama bin Laden**

The architect of 9/11, whose ideological war reshaped global conflict and defined a generation's fears. His attack is the hinge between 20th- and 21st-century war.

War/Period: GWOT catalyst. **Appears:** Ch. 11–12. **Also:** Shadow war origins.

45. **William Westmoreland**

Vietnam commander who pursued an attrition strategy rooted in WWII logic, failing to realize that firepower cannot kill an idea. His name is tied to the body-count era.

War/Period: Vietnam. **Appears:** Ch. 6 (implicit). **Also:** Attrition doctrine.

46. **Pop Warner**

The football strategist whose innovations influenced early military thinking on discipline and aggression. He appears in NTOT as a cultural architect of toughness.

War/Period: Early 20th-century sports era. **Appears:** Ch. 2. **Also:** Sports pipeline.

47. **Richard Nixon**

The president who inherited a war he could not end and pursued "peace with honor," revealing how political survival and national will can diverge fatally.

War/Period: Vietnam → Cold War. **Appears:** Ch. 6. **Also:** Strategic collapse.

48. **George Stevens**

WWII filmmaker whose footage documented Dachau's liberation, confronting the world with undeniable evidence of atrocity.

War/Period: WWII. **Appears:** Ch. 1. **Also:** Visual memory archive.

49. **Harry Truman**

The president who ended WWII with atomic fire and began the containment doctrine. His decisions created the Cold War terrain Vietnam grew out of.

War/Period: WWII → Korea → Cold War. **Appears:** Context Ch. 6. **Also:** Strategic inheritance.

50. **Jim Thorpe**

Perhaps the greatest athlete in American history, Thorpe's clash with Eisenhower symbolizes the link between indigenous identity, physical grit, and national mythology.

War/Period: Pre-WWI American culture. **Appears:** Ch. 2. **Also:** Identity and resilience.

51. **Nick Turse**

The historian who revealed the Vietnam War Crimes Working Group files, proving that atrocity was systemic rather than exceptional. Turse forced America to confront what it tried to forget.

War/Period: Vietnam (retrospective). **Appears:** Ch. 6. **Also:** Systemic atrocity.

52. **Deborah Nelson**

The journalist who traced buried war-crimes investigations, giving voice to victims whose stories never reached official records.

War/Period: Vietnam (investigative). **Appears:** Ch. 6. **Also:** Hidden truth.

53. **Tim O'Brien**

The Vietnam veteran who turned memory into mythic truth. His stories, half-real and half-confession, carry the emotional weight of an entire generation.

War/Period: Vietnam. **Appears:** Ch. 15. **Also:** Veteran storytelling.

54. **Colin Powell**

A Soldier-scholar who emerged from Vietnam's ambiguity committed to clarity, later shaping the Gulf War with overwhelming force doctrine.

War/Period: Vietnam → Gulf War. **Appears:** Context Ch. 10. **Also:** Strategic restraint.

55. **Norman Schwarzkopf**

The architect of Desert Storm, Schwarzkopf's crushing victory against Iraq reinforced the illusion of risk-free war for a new generation.

War/Period: Gulf War. **Appears:** Ch. 10. **Also:** Precision warfare narrative.

56. **George Marshall**

The general who not only won WWII but rebuilt Europe afterward. Marshall understood that victory without compassion breeds new wars.

War/Period: WWII → Cold War. **Appears:** Context Ch. 1, 6. **Also:** Leadership legacy.

57. **Curtis LeMay**

The general whose firebombing campaigns killed hundreds of thousands, shaping airpower doctrine and the moral debates that still haunt strategic bombing.

War/Period: WWII → Cold War. **Appears:** Ch. 4–5. **Also:** Strategic destruction.

58. **Omar Bradley**

A steady, soft-spoken general whose leadership in Europe contrasted with the flamboyance of others. Bradley represents the quiet professionalism of the era.

War/Period: WWII. **Appears:** Contextual WWII leadership. **Also:** Ethical contrast.

59. **Erwin Rommel**

The Desert Fox, whose brilliance forced Allied commanders to adapt rapidly. Rommel appears as a symbol of enemy competence and tragedy.

War/Period: WWII (North Africa, Normandy). **Appears:** Contextual in Ch. 4. **Also:** Enemy command ethos.

60. **Hideki Tojo**

Japan's wartime prime minister whose militaristic zeal fueled invasions across Asia and crimes against civilians. Tojo's leadership represents the lethal fusion of nationalism, fanaticism, and power.

War/Period: WWII (Pacific Theater). **Appears:** Implied in Pacific war discussion. **Also:** Imperial militarism.

61. **Isoroku Yamamoto**

The naval strategist behind the Pearl Harbor attack, Yamamoto understood both America's strengths and its potential wrath. His gamble awakened a superior enemy and altered the course of world history.

War/Period: WWII (Pacific). **Appears:** Contextually in Ch. 4. **Also:** Strategic shock analysis.

62. **Douglas MacArthur**

The iconic and controversial general of WWII's Pacific front and the Korean War. MacArthur's ambition, brilliance, and defiance of civilian oversight illustrate the fragile balance between military command and democratic authority.

War/Period: WWII → Korea. **Appears:** Contextual in ROE/civil–military power. **Also:** Command responsibility lessons.

63. **Harry S. Truman**

The president who ended WWII with atomic fire and launched the global containment strategy that shaped the Cold War. His decisions laid the geopolitical groundwork that ultimately produced Korea and Vietnam.

War/Period: WWII → Korean War → Early Cold War. **Appears:** Contextually in Ch. 6. **Also:** Strategic inheritance.

64. **Joseph Goebbels**

Hitler's propaganda minister who weaponized film, radio, and myth into a machine of obedience. Goebbels demonstrates how narrative can become deadlier than any weapon.

War/Period: WWII. **Appears:** Ch. 5 (propaganda system). **Also:** Information warfare parallels.

65. **Heinrich Himmler**

The cold bureaucrat of genocide, Himmler engineered the SS and oversaw the extermination apparatus that murdered millions. He embodies the horror of cruelty carried out through paperwork and procedure.

War/Period: WWII/Holocaust. **Appears:** Ch. 5 (implicitly). **Also:** Bureaucratic mass murder.

66. **Reinhard Heydrich**

The architect of the Wannsee Conference whose precision and brutality made him feared across Europe. Heydrich's assassination remains one of WWII's defining acts of resistance.

War/Period: WWII. **Appears:** Contextual in Ch. 5. **Also:** State violence mechanisms.

67. **Hannah Arendt**

The philosopher who introduced "the banality of evil," arguing that everyday people can commit atrocities when systems reward obedience. Her insight forms part of NTOT's ethical foundation.

War/Period: Post-WWII. **Appears:** Implied in Ch. 5. **Also:** Moral philosophy of atrocity.

68. **Václav Havel**

A dissident playwright who confronted Soviet power with truth rather than violence. Havel shows that moral courage can outlast empires.

War/Period: Cold War, Eastern Bloc. **Appears:** Philosophically tied to Ch. 5. **Also:** Resistance leadership.

69. **Aleksandr Solzhenitsyn**

The Soviet dissident whose *Gulag Archipelago* exposed the machinery of communist repression. Solzhenitsyn is a reminder that tyranny thrives when truth is forbidden.

War/Period: Cold War, Soviet terror. **Appears:** Implied in Ch. 5. **Also:** State violence testimony.

70. **Edward Lansdale**

The CIA operative whose unconventional warfare strategies shaped early U.S. action in Vietnam. Lansdale was a romantic idealist in a war that crushed idealism.

War/Period: Vietnam (1950s–60s). **Appears:** Contextually in Ch. 6. **Also:** COIN origins.

71. **General Võ Nguyên Giáp**

The strategist who defeated both France and the United States, proving that willpower and patience can overcome superior firepower. Giáp remains one of the greatest asymmetric commanders in history.

War/Period: First Indochina → Vietnam. **Appears:** Implied in Ch. 6. **Also:** Asymmetric strategy model.

72. **Le Ly Hayslip**

A Vietnamese civilian who survived both sides of the war and wrote her truth into existence. Her memoirs reveal the human cost beneath every flag and ideology.

War/Period: Vietnam (civilian experience). **Appears:** Thematically fits Ch. 6–7. **Also:** Civilian trauma lens.

73. **Saloth Sar (Pol Pot)**

The schoolteacher who became architect of the Cambodian Genocide, proving how ideology mixed with paranoia can become one of history's deadliest forces.

War/Period: Cambodia, 1975–1979. **Appears:** Ch. 5. **Also:** Extremism and mass murder.

74. **Mullah Mohammad Omar**

The solitary cleric who built the Taliban through austere ideology and absolute control. Under his rule, Afghanistan became the seedbed for al-Qaeda and the 9/11 attack.

War/Period: Afghanistan/Taliban rule. **Appears:** Ch. 12 (context). **Also:** Insurgency foundations.

75. **Abu Musab al-Zarqawi**

    The Jordanian extremist whose brutality in Iraq laid the groundwork for ISIS. Zarqawi turned sectarian violence into strategy.

    War/Period: Iraq War insurgency. **Appears:** Contextually in Ch. 12. **Also:** Rise of ISIS.

76. **Anwar al-Awlaki**

    A charismatic cleric whose online sermons radicalized thousands, demonstrating how modern jihad spreads through pixels instead of camps.

    War/Period: GWOT (2000s). **Appears:** Contextual backdrop. **Also:** Digital-era radicalization.

77. **Abu Bakr al-Baghdadi**

    The founder of ISIS's caliphate, Baghdadi exploited chaos in Iraq and Syria to build a terror state. His ascent shows how power fills vacuums left by broken nations.

    War/Period: Iraq/Syria (ISIS era). **Appears:** Conceptually Ch. 12. **Also:** Terror-state doctrine.

78. **Saif al-Adel**

A former Egyptian special forces officer turned al-Qaeda strategist, al-Adel symbolizes the merger of professional military skill and extremist ideology.

War/Period: Al-Qaeda. **Appears:** Contextual GWOT analysis. **Also:** Terror strategy evolution.

79. **Prince Bandar bin Sultan**

A Saudi diplomat who shaped Cold War proxy conflicts and later U.S.–Middle East relations. Bandar's role shows how diplomacy, intelligence, and shadow warfare intertwine.

War/Period: Cold War → GWOT. **Appears:** Contextually. **Also:** Alliance politics.

80. **David Petraeus**

The general behind the Iraq "Surge," Petraeus attempted to reframe counterinsurgency as a humane, population-focused strategy. His rise and fall reflect the volatility of modern confidence in military saviors.

War/Period: Iraq War. **Appears:** Implicit in Ch. 12. **Also:** COIN doctrine legacy.

81. **Stanley McChrystal**

Architect of JSOC's man-hunting operations, McChrystal fused intelligence and operations into a single lethal rhythm. His work demonstrates the razor's edge between precision and moral overreach.

War/Period: GWOT. **Appears:** Conceptually referenced. **Also:** Special operations evolution.

82. **Mike Durant**

    The Black Hawk pilot captured in Mogadishu whose broken body and resilience became emblematic of the battle's brutality. Durant represents the human cost of small wars with big consequences.

    War/Period: Somalia, 1993. **Appears:** Ch. 11 (context). **Also:** POW reality.

83. **Frances Slanger**

    The first American nurse killed by enemy fire in Europe, Slanger's compassion under bombardment became a symbol of wartime sacrifice among medics and caregivers.

    War/Period: WWII (Europe). **Appears:** Ch. 4. **Also:** Humanitarian courage.

84. **Karl Marlantes**

    A Marine whose novel *Matterhorn* and memoir *What It Is Like to Go to War* capture Vietnam's emotional terrain. Marlantes is a guide to the interior battle no medal can measure.

    War/Period: Vietnam. **Appears:** Thematically tied to Ch. 15. **Also:** Internal war insight.

85. **David Halberstam**

The journalist who exposed Vietnam's strategic illusions and later wrote *The Best and the Brightest*, chronicling the hubris of America's elite decision-makers.

War/Period: Vietnam. **Appears:** Contextually in Ch. 6. **Also:** Policy critique.

86. **James Mattis**

A Marine general whose intellect and discipline earned respect across political divides. Mattis embodied restraint and clarity at a time when modern war demanded both.

War/Period: Iraq/Afghanistan. **Appears:** Implied leadership influence. **Also:** Ethical command.

87. **Condoleezza Rice**

National Security Advisor and Secretary of State during the early GWOT, Rice shaped the diplomatic architecture of America's long wars.

War/Period: GWOT. **Appears:** Contextually Ch. 12. **Also:** Decision-making under crisis.

88. **Hillary Rodham Clinton**

Senator during the Iraq War authorization and later Secretary of State. Clinton's decisions reflect the political complexities shaping America's intervention calculus.

War/Period: GWOT political era. **Appears:** Implicitly. **Also:** Policy debates.

89. **John McCain**

Navy pilot, POW survivor, and senator who became a moral voice against torture and extremism. McCain symbolizes endurance and the cost of captivity.

War/Period: Vietnam. **Appears:** Conceptually. **Also:** POW legacy.

90. **William Calley**

The platoon leader held responsible for the My Lai massacre, Calley remains one of the most painful symbols of war's moral collapse.

War/Period: Vietnam. **Appears:** Ch. 6 (implicitly). **Also:** Atrocity context.

91. **Saddam Hussein**

The Iraqi dictator whose invasion of Kuwait triggered Desert Storm and whose downfall reshaped the Middle East. His regime became the focal point of early GWOT objectives.

War/Period: Gulf War → Iraq War. **Appears:** Ch. 10, 12. **Also:** Geopolitical catalyst.

92. **Muammar Gaddafi**

Libyan strongman whose sponsorship of terror foreshadowed modern asymmetric conflict. His fall demonstrated the chaos unleashed by regime change without plan.

War/Period: Cold War → GWOT. **Appears:** Contextually. **Also:** Intervention cost.

93. **Benjamin Netanyahu**

The Israeli leader whose doctrine of deterrence, security, and counterterror operations reflects the complexity of modern asymmetric conflict.

War/Period: Modern Middle East. **Appears:** Contextually. **Also:** Strategic parallels.

94. **Ariel Sharon**

An Israeli general turned prime minister whose career spanned armored warfare, counterinsurgency, and political upheaval. Sharon's decisions influence modern debates on urban warfare.

War/Period: Arab–Israeli wars → 2000s. **Appears:** Contextually. **Also:** ROE discussions.

95. **Abdul Sattar Abu Risha**

The tribal leader who helped ignite the Anbar Awakening, turning Sunni tribes against al-Qaeda. His actions demonstrated that alliances, not firepower, decide insurgencies.

War/Period: Iraq War. **Appears:** Implicit in Ch. 12. **Also:** Tribal politics.

96. **King Abdullah II of Jordan**

    A monarch shaped by regional conflict, Abdullah balances security and diplomacy in a region defined by instability. His voice offers perspective from a nation between war and survival.

    War/Period: Modern Middle East. **Appears:** Contextually. **Also:** Coalition dynamics.

97. **Lloyd Austin**

    A commander in Iraq who oversaw crucial transitions and withdrawals, Austin's career reflects the burden of ending wars rather than winning them.

    War/Period: Iraq War. **Appears:** Conceptually. **Also:** Civil–military execution.

98. **Michael Flynn**

    An intelligence officer whose later political radicalization illustrates the dangers of fractured trust between military truth and public narrative.

    War/Period: GWOT → post-service. **Appears:** Thematically in Ch. 13. **Also:** Civil–military risks.

99. **Vladimir Putin**

The architect of the 2022 invasion of Ukraine, proving authoritarian ambition doesn't fade with time—it bides its time. Putin stands as the modern echo of 20th-century aggression.

War/Period: Russia–Ukraine. **Appears:** Epilogue. **Also:** Failure of deterrence.

100. **Xi Jinping**

Leader of modern China whose fusion of surveillance, nationalism, and military expansion marks the new frontier of global authoritarianism. Xi represents the rising challenge at the center of 21st-century conflict.

War/Period: China (2012–present). **Appears:** Conceptual backdrop. **Also:** Future conflict paradigm.

Books and Official Reports

Alford, Matthew, and Tom Secker. National Security Cinema: The Shocking New Evidence of Government Control in Hollywood. Scotts Valley, CA: CreateSpace Independent Publishing, 2017.

Anderson, Lars. Carlisle vs. Army: Jim Thorpe, Dwight Eisenhower, Pop Warner, and the Forgotten Story of Football's Greatest Battle. New York: Random House, 2007.

Appy, Christian G. Working-Class War: American Combat Soldiers and Vietnam. Chapel Hill: University of North Carolina Press, 1993.

Arendt, Hannah. Eichmann in Jerusalem: A Report on the Banality of Evil. New York: Viking Press, 1963.

Arendt, Hannah. The Origins of Totalitarianism. New York: Harcourt, Brace & Company, 1951.

Bacevich, Andrew J. The New American Militarism: How Americans Are Seduced by War. New York: Oxford University Press, 2005.

Bowden, Mark. Black Hawk Down: A Story of Modern War. New York: Atlantic Monthly Press, 1999.

Brokaw, Tom. The Greatest Generation. New York: Random House, 1998.

Brown University, Watson Institute for International and Public Affairs. Costs of War Project: U.S. and Allied War Deaths and Costs, 2001–2025. Providence, RI: Brown University, 2025.

Brown University, Watson Institute. AI and Modern Warfare Briefing. Providence, RI: Brown University, 2023.

Bush, George W. "Address to a Joint Session of Congress and the American People." Washington, DC, September 20, 2001.

Caputo, Philip. A Rumor of War. New York: Holt, Rinehart and Winston, 1977.

Center for Army Lessons Learned (CALL). Escalation of Force (EOF) Tactics, Techniques, and Procedures. CALL Handbook

07-21. Fort Leavenworth, KS: U.S. Army Combined Arms Center, 2007.

Chairman of the Joint Chiefs of Staff. CJCSI 3121.01B: Standing Rules of Engagement / Standing Rules for the Use of Force for U.S. Forces. Washington, DC, 2005.

Department of the Army and U.S. Marine Corps. FM 6-27 / MCTP 11-10C: The Commander's Handbook on the Law of Land Warfare. Washington, DC, 2019.

Department of Defense. Department of Defense Law of War Manual. Washington, DC, June 2015; updated July 2023.

Department of Defense. Electronic Barrier and "McNamara's Line" Reports. Washington, DC: DoD Historical Office, 1967–1968.

Department of Defense. Operation Enduring Freedom and Operation Iraqi Freedom: Casualty Summary. Washington, DC, 2024.

Department of Veterans Affairs. National Veteran Suicide Prevention Annual Report. Washington, DC, 2024.

Farrell, John A. Richard Nixon: The Life. New York: Doubleday, 2017.

Fick, Nathaniel. One Bullet Away: The Making of a Marine Officer. Boston: Houghton Mifflin, 2005.

Fitzgerald, Frances. Fire in the Lake: The Vietnamese and the Americans in Vietnam. New York: Vintage Books, 1972.

GAO (U.S. Government Accountability Office). Capitol Security: Review of Events of January 6, 2021. GAO-22-104829. Washington, DC, 2022.

Greiner, Bernd. War Without Fronts: The USA in Vietnam. New York: Yale University Press, 2009.

Hedges, Chris. War Is a Force That Gives Us Meaning. New York: PublicAffairs, 2002.

Herring, George C. America's Longest War: The United States and Vietnam, 1950–1975. 6th ed. New York: McGraw-Hill, 2020.

Hoffer, Eric. The True Believer: Thoughts on the Nature of Mass Movements. New York: Harper & Brothers, 1951.

Hughes, Ken. Chasing Shadows: The Nixon Tapes, the Chennault Affair, and the Origins of Watergate. Charlottesville: University of Virginia Press, 2014.

Illinois Army National Guard. Force Protection and Rules of Engagement Policy Directive No. 16-02. Springfield, IL, 2016.

Jenkins, Tricia. The CIA in Hollywood: How the Agency Shapes Film and Television. Austin: University of Texas Press, 2012.

Karnow, Stanley. Vietnam: A History. New York: Penguin Books, 1997.

Krakauer, Jon. Where Men Win Glory: The Odyssey of Pat Tillman. New York: Doubleday, 2009.

Lawrence, Mark Atwood. Assuming the Burden: Europe and the American Commitment to War in Vietnam. Berkeley: University of California Press, 2005.

Le Bon, Gustave. The Crowd: A Study of the Popular Mind. London: T. Fisher Unwin, 1895.

Levi, Primo. If This Is a Man. Translated by Stuart Woolf. New York: Orion Press, 1959.

Logevall, Fredrik. Embers of War: The Fall of an Empire and the Making of America's Vietnam. New York: Random House, 2012.

McMaster, H. R. Dereliction of Duty: Lyndon Johnson, Robert McNamara, the Joint Chiefs of Staff, and the Lies That Led to Vietnam. New York: HarperCollins, 1997.

McNamara, Robert S., and James G. Blight. Argument Without End: In Search of Answers to the Vietnam Tragedy. New York: PublicAffairs, 1999.

National Archives and Records Administration (NARA). Vietnam War Crimes Working Group Files. College Park, MD, 1994.

National Security Archive. The "Chennault Affair": Declassified Documents on the 1968 Vietnam Peace Talks. Washington, DC: George Washington University, 2016–2017.

Pew Research Center. The Civil–Military Gap: War and Sacrifice in the Post-9/11 Era. Washington, DC, October 5, 2011.

Prados, John. Vietnam: The History of an Unwinnable War, 1945–1975. Lawrence, KS: University Press of Kansas, 2009.

Rawls, John. A Theory of Justice. Cambridge, MA: Harvard University Press, 1971.

Ricks, Thomas E. Fiasco: The American Military Adventure in Iraq. New York: Penguin Press, 2006.

Sirvent, Roberto. The Militarization of U.S. Sports. Providence, RI: Watson Institute, Brown University, 2025.

Suitt, Thomas. High Suicide Rates among United States Service Members and Veterans of the Post-9/11 Wars. Providence, RI: Brown University, Watson Institute, 2021.

Tocqueville, Alexis de. Democracy in America. Paris: Charles Gosselin, 1835.

Tregaskis, Richard. Guadalcanal Diary. New York: Random House, 1943.

Turse, Nick. Kill Anything That Moves: The Real American War in Vietnam. New York: Metropolitan Books, 2013.

U.S. Army Center of Military History. United States Army in World War II (The Green Books). Washington, DC: Government Printing Office, 1946–1978.

Vietnam Veterans Against the War. The Winter Soldier Investigation. Boston: Beacon Press, 1972.

Weigley, Russell F. The American Way of War. Bloomington: Indiana University Press, 1973.

Welch, Bob. American Nightingale: The Story of Frances Slanger, Forgotten Heroine of Normandy. New York: Atria Books, 2004.

Wiesel, Elie. Night. Translated by Marion Wiesel. New York: Farrar, Straus and Giroux, 2006.

Woodward, Bob. Plan of Attack. New York: Simon & Schuster, 2004.

Articles and Journals

Hoge, Charles W., et al. "Combat Duty in Iraq and Afghanistan, Mental Health Problems, and Barriers to Care." New England Journal of Medicine 351, no. 1 (2004): 13–22.

Litz, Brett T., and Shira Maguen. "Moral Injury in Veterans of War." PTSD Research Quarterly 23, no. 1 (2012): 1–6.

Reger, Mark A., et al. "Suicide Mortality and Firearm Deaths Among Veterans and Active-Duty Service Members, 2001–2022." JAMA Network Open 6, no. 8 (2023): e2328843.

Warner, Dana M., and Susan J. Appel. "Post-9/11 Families and Secondary Trauma." Journal of Family Social Work 23, no. 4 (2020): 317–336.

Films and Cultural Works

28 Days Later. Directed by Danny Boyle. Fox Searchlight Pictures, 2002.

28 Weeks Later. Directed by Juan Carlos Fresnadillo. Fox Searchlight Pictures, 2007.

American Sniper. Directed by Clint Eastwood. Warner Bros., 2014.

Band of Brothers. Directed by Steven Spielberg and Tom Hanks. HBO, 2001.

Black Hawk Down. Directed by Ridley Scott. Columbia Pictures, 2001.

Born on the Fourth of July. Directed by Oliver Stone. Universal Pictures, 1989.

Fahrenheit 451. Directed by François Truffaut. United Artists, 1966.

Full Metal Jacket. Directed by Stanley Kubrick. Warner Bros., 1987.

In the Valley of Elah. Directed by Paul Haggis. Warner Independent Pictures, 2007.

Lone Survivor. Directed by Peter Berg. Universal Pictures, 2013.

Night of the Living Dead. Directed by George A. Romero. Image Ten, 1968.

Platoon. Directed by Oliver Stone. Orion Pictures, 1986.

Saving Private Ryan. Directed by Steven Spielberg. DreamWorks, 1998.

Sands of Iwo Jima. Directed by Allan Dwan. Republic Pictures, 1949.

The Deer Hunter. Directed by Michael Cimino. Universal Pictures, 1978.

The Green Berets. Directed by John Wayne and Ray Kellogg. Warner Bros., 1968.

The Thin Red Line. Directed by Terrence Malick. 20th Century Fox, 1998.

Top Gun. Directed by Tony Scott. Paramount Pictures, 1986.

We Were Soldiers. Directed by Randall Wallace. Paramount Pictures, 2002.

Zero Dark Thirty. Directed by Kathryn Bigelow. Columbia Pictures, 2012.

www.ingramcontent.com/pod-product-compliance
Lightning Source LLC
LaVergne TN
LVHW090514110826
845146LV00003B/853

* 9 7 9 8 9 9 3 6 4 3 9 0 8 *